Stories of Sudden Sex

Explicit Dirty Sex Collection for Horny Adults - Bisexual, Milfs, Anal Sex, Gangbang, Lesbian, Thresome, BDSM and Much More

Oscar Birchfield

rendering of legal, financial, medical or professional advice. The content within this book has been derived from various sources. Please consult a licensed professional before attempting any techniques outlined in this book.

By reading this document, the reader agrees that under no circumstances is the author responsible for any losses, direct or indirect, that are incurred as a result of the use of the information contained within this document, including, but not limited to, errors, omissions, or inaccuracies.

Table of Contents

KISS MY ASS

The doorbell rang. Sebastian checked the clock and put his book down on the table just beside his couch. Heather was on time this time. A week ago, she was late by thirteen minutes, and he had left her standing outside for almost half an hour, before listening to her excuses for being late. She had an extended shift at the supermarket which eventually resulted in missing the train. Sebastian had listened to her story, but was too defiant to continue her training that day. They despised that. In any case, Sebastian knew that Heather would be back. As it was her first time in his dungeon, Heather begged and argued, apprehensive that he would not accept her, train her and help her fulfill her twisted fantasies.

Heather had the brilliant spark of natural beauty, temptation and elegance. Her thick, long, dense and blonde hair streamed behind her like the continuous waves of a waterfall. Her skin was beautiful, radiant and shone like molten gold, abundant like rich milk and cream. She possessed a statuesque shape in her tall, buxom, curvy framework with breasts the size of melons. Her ass was crafted from marble to perfection - two large mounds resembling the perfectly hemispherical scoops of ice creams, a mesmerizing and an attractive BIG BEAUTIFUL WOMAN.

Sebastian, Heather's immediate boss in the supermarket, whenever would see them in her tight, shape fitting skirt, he would always drool to devour them that way and even spurt condiments all over that juicy booty to eat off for all day. Being a mommy of two little kids, she had a lot on her shoulders and fulfilling her twisted fantasies was just a way to release off all her tensions.

Heather's first time with her boss was brutal, yet overwhelming experience for her. She just thought a little peek-a-boo and a little temptation with a touch of mischief would help her secure her job. Well, indeed she secured her job, but in the process, she started to yearn for more. When Sebastian took this divorced MILF, used her for his pleasure like a toy, Heather was unable to think. All she could do was to feel and be lost in the moment where she lost herself experiencing orgasms one after another. Sebastian marked her as his, claimed her, and finally owned her. The next time when Heather thought to express her gratitude for her job to Sebastian, it was more severe than her first time. Sebastian had practically ruined the chance of any other man in her life. He had induced in her mind the joy of surrender, the pleasure to be controlled by a dominant that brought forth the naughty kitten in her and fed her like a wolf. He gave her what she was afraid to ask for, somewhat embarrassed to ask for.

While for Heather, she desired for every inch of her boss, the smell of his breath on her needing lips, the taste of him and his voice rummaging through every vein in her body. There was no turning back for Heather.

As Heather was late on her first interaction in his dungeon, Sebastian had slammed the door on her face. But after repeated pleadings and desperate begging, Sebastian replied to her emails and messages. After two days of begging messages, he finally permitted her to return once again, a week after her first scheduled appointment. Moreover, she would pay a price for her misjudgment. Sebastian hadn't replied any further to her messages, irrespective of the fact that Heather continued sending messages after messages expressing her gratitude and happiness. When she finally understood, he wasn't going to reply to her any further, she was somewhat heartbroken and even thought him to be arrogant and heartless.

Finally, there they were; Heather was waiting impatiently to enter his dungeon, Sebastian was waiting eagerly to bind her body and free her mind; patiently waiting to tease her with his gentle touch and tempt her with his rough ones. Sebastian checked through the peephole. The thirty six-year-old curvaceous woman with deep, dense and long blonde hair, enormous green-colored eyes, mesmerizing enough to captivate anyone's senses and pierce through the soul accompanied with a flawless face. But today her gorgeousness was somewhat distorted with stress, and perhaps a little terrified. He left her standing there for about ten minutes, enjoying the most of her subtle looks around, anxious glances and her silent begging for the door to open. Amazingly, she remained still and didn't press the doorbell more than once. Sebastian chuckled as he was denied from the exquisite opportunity to add to her demerits.

At last, he opened the door and asked, "Hey slut, how may I help you?"

Heather gulped. Her lips trembled as his words struck the chord in her heart. She shivered as his peering eyes feasted on her lush body. "Why does he act so naive to my plights? Why is it that he always wants me at his mercy? Why does it always arouse me so much even when I hate it sometimes?" Thoughts crowded her restless mind. Every time she was near him, her thoughts got messy; just thinking of him, looking at him, smelling him. The sound of his name inflamed her lust. When she saw him chuckling again, she panicked, not to gain any further demerit, "I came to meet you and to..." Heather replied in a lovely voice, yet it resonated like a desperate whisper.

"Speak up, slut," he said. "Why are you here?"

Sebastian looked with intense satisfaction as the nervousness and embarrassment played over her face.

Heather glanced around anxiously before answering. "I...I've come," she took a quick glance of the corridor environment of the apartment, swallowed hard and completed, "for my t...t...training." The words got out. As her dreaded expressions conquered her face, anybody could surmise how concerned, she was regarding the thickness of the walls in the apartment.

Sebastian's dungeon was a private apartment in the 30-storied Tribeca Tower, one of the biggest structures in the city. When Heather reached her destination called The Mystique Dungeon, she couldn't believe how such a strange place could be located in a posh neighborhood. The apartments in the building were so luxurious that Heather felt her stay in here for a couple of hours would feel as if she were staying in her own home; so elegant, so pleasurable. She also believed that the well-furnished apartment building provided its dwellers with all they needed to enjoy a comfortable and extravagant living with little or no interference. She further fascinated that the dungeon on the topmost floor of the building would undoubtedly offer an incredible view of the city's horizon.

Sebastian showed Heather no mercy; this was

included as a disciplinary technique for missing her first appointment.

"I'm sorry, I didn't get that," Sebastian exclaimed too boisterously. "Training? What sort of training?" He heard a stifled laugh from the next door. So had Heather, and her eyes widened, and an extreme flush surged over her face and neck. For a moment, Heather heard her heart pounding like bass drums. She was yearning the touch of her boss and her master. There was something unexplainable about his strong hands. Whenever he had gripped her in the past with savage lust and raw passion, she felt so secure and wanted. It was pure bliss. And Heather was desperate for his touch again. On the other hand, Sebastian's investigating eyes never missed those subtle expressions that always tempted his mind. He wondered how much far her voice could expand. He was soon going to discover.

Heather looked at Sebastian pleadingly. He just gazed at her, finally giving an exaggerated addressing tilt to his head; however, there was none on his face.

She alarmingly looked at the door to his right, and after that gazed down the stairs turning her head. Then her frightened, yet sparkling eyes met his. But his eyes simply drilled into hers with the message. "Indeed, you should."

"I'm here for my sex training." Heather asserted firmly, but not as noisy as he had been while questioning her.

"That's neither what I do, nor what you seek. So, let's begin once again. Correctly this time, shall we? Why are you here slut?" Sebastian questioned firmly.

Sebastian could see the widespread agitation and emotional outrage all over her face. In any case, just within seconds, he could sense her recalling what it had been like when she felt that she had demolished her once in a lifetime opportunity on her first endeavor, and the tremendous relief and boundless bliss when she got the email of second and last chance. Her face transcended to one of sheer determination. "Do it, Heather? Overcome your shyness. Only he knows your secret desires. Only he has seen your hidden passions. He's the only one whom you can completely trust, devote absolutely and love admirably. Only with him, you're free. So just let your fears go." Her mind screamed in her ears and she heard it resonating in her soul.

"I'm here for my slut training," Heather stated in a full voice. The modesty in her tone restricted it from being a hysterical scream.

"Bravo, dear. There is a punishment for making such a poor start." Sebastian asserted. "You will strip here in the corridor. Totally. So STRIP."

The sudden indescribable terror was back in her eyes. She anxiously gazed the corridor from the corner of her eyes, and then her head turned back to check the full wall of doors downstairs. "Should I do what he's asking me to do?" Heather wondered inwardly. She shivered as chills gushed down her spine. However, she realized she needed to follow his orders or else her repeated mailings, messages, and his permission for her return, her standing in front of his front door would yield no result. "Heather, this is what you're here for. You want him to explore your darker sides, to illuminate it. You want him to show you every twisted, frightening thought you ever had. If you want his eyes burning your skin, don't turn back. If you want his words tearing your mind apart, well, this is the time." Heather shivered like a leaf in a storm as thoughts crowded her perverted mind. It simply made her blush more in embarrassment, she felt her cheeks burning or was it his fierce eyes burning her cheeks? Heather gulped, and then with trembling hands, she gradually unbuttoned her blouse and let it follow gravity. The faint sound of her blouse toppling down onto the floor, just made it worse for her and she felt her heart in her throat. As for Sebastian, he gazed in delighted amazement as her blush covered her upper chest, and though lighter, vanished under the edge of her bra.

Heather fumbled with the buttons of her skirt, her fingers were icy cold, her heart was pounding in her throat, and she was shaking so terribly; Sebastian's eyes continued feasting on the incredible sight. Heather began to drive her skirt down as she wiggled her hip and ass. And as they cleared her panties, there was a sudden click of a door lock, and her frightened eyes darted to the door adjacent to her man. Heather's eyes widened, Sebastian just chuckled mischievously. There was also a muffled moan from the next door. Sebastian could easily recognize it from one of the keyholes from the next door. It resulted in a tight grin on his lips. Consequently, her blush grew even more profound, her ordeal was taking a toll on her mind and body.

Heather understood then that the longer she took to strip the more she would bear those prying eyes in the corridor. She pushed the skirt down and off her legs, taking her heels with them. She was yet to kick away the heels before her icy fingers snaked to her back to unhook her bra. She slipped out of it rapidly, and rushed for her panties, and flung them down and off. She was almost off-balance and could have easily tumbled onto the floor, but her reflexes grabbed the wall balancing her. There were suppressed rhythmic moans and giggles that escaped from the door beside Sebastian's. Clearly, the eager viewer's hand was stuffed in his or her mouth.

Acknowledging what she needed to do, Heather stood straight, hands clenched in a fist next to her. This was it. This was Heather's new beginning. This was her new ending. Her expressive and sparkling eyes measured the length of the man feasting on her lush seduction. A man in a blue checked suit, complete with a grey shirt, silver tie, and dark short hair devouring the savage beauty standing right in front of him. He couldn't believe it if this was his day. He just wanted to tightly embrace her in his arms and freeze till eternity. But he was in charge, he was in control. Heather's entire body ignited as Sebastian clenched his jaw. She just stripped in front of him, but his peering eyes were stripping her soul. When their eyes locked, something electric tingled across the flesh in between her legs. "What was that? Terror? Arousal? Pleasure?" Heather's mind was messed up. Something inside her mind screamed and warned her, "This man is a devil, Heather? He sins like a devil. You tasted his animalistic kisses. Beware!" Heather gulped.

Sebastian was amazed to see the nervousness playing all over his girl. She was so ravishing, like a butterfly, so pretty to see, yet choosy to land on a flower. She let him in, yearned for him, and wanted him. Sebastian was bewildered as his words fell short to describe her beauty. He just wanted all of her, her flaws, her smiles, her mistakes, her rights, her jokes, her everything. He just lusted for her. Sebastian's lips twitched just a little as Heather sucked in a breath. He placed his hands on her shoulder, his fingers long and strong, and his touch so full of warmth. The way he gazed at her and devoured her seduction was too much for Heather. She shivered when her perverted mind screamed to retaliate her fears, "I don't care if he's a devil because his eyes are heaven. I don't care if his kisses are animalistic because his passionate touch made me feel alive. I love it when he consumes me. I love it when he devours me, it's so electric. Even if I try to run, I cannot because I'm in his Venus flytrap. I'm his."

Sebastian leaned forward and whispered in her ears, "Welcome to my den, kitten! Say hello to your Master!" He then gestured, and ventured back, and waved her into the room. As Sebastian shut the front door, he heard another door creaking to close and clatter fiercely. He grinned mischievously; he wasn't the only one rejoicing his new whore's embarrassment. He turned back into the room after locking the door. He saw a youthful woman, a divorced MILF, a BIG BEAUTIFUL WOMAN before him, biting her lip. He wanted and need Heather in his life. It didn't matter how. He felt his heart pounding like bass drums. For a moment, Sebastian felt dreaming, it was all his imagination, he was losing his mind. He wanted to watch her walk in and out of the room, naked, just so he could feel how he did when he first saw her; when he first saw the beautiful smile striking a chord in his heart, those juicy lips, and dark excited eyes. As for Heather, she didn't like the idea that her garments were left in the corridor for all to see. Sebastian regained his composure while adjusting the twitching erection feeding on testosterone; he then simply turned and strolled into the living room, and settled down in his seat. Heather followed him.

She was puzzled about what to do next, or where to stand. Sebastian found her watching curiously, yet nervously the environment in the room. She didn't see anything strange unless she found the innumerable shelves on the walls. Her eyes finally settled on the long footstool just in front of Sebastian. There on the table lay several papers.

Finally, his watchful eyes met her sparkling ones. "Kneel beside the table, knees wide. Put your hands behind your back." Sebastian commanded.

In spite of having stripped in almost publicly, and standing naked in a stranger's apartment corridor, Heather hesitated for a moment. It was as if beyond her strength to adapt. Gradually she moved toward the table and brought herself down to her knees. Her trembling hands went to her back where one hand softly griped another. She felt her icy cold fingers on her other hand; she shivered when an electric sensation gushed down her spine producing a tingling effect in between her legs. Heather sensed herself moistening. Sebastian could see her mind battling against her muscles as she gradually parted her knees, yet not sufficiently wide enough to please him. He kept her in that submissive position for almost five minutes for her to realize she had done enough.

"Are you deaf and dumb, slut?" He said as he locked his furious eyes to her submissive ones. "I said knees spread wide, not simply parted." He said it without command or hostility. His voice seemed like that of a daddy dictating his girl; obviously, he had learned and experienced that dominance over years of practice.

Gradually, biting her lip once more, Heather parted her knees further apart. She watched her ardent taker for a sign, but he gave her none. Then, when her knees started to strain her muscles and thighs, Sebastian spoke.

"This is the position you will take whenever you're in my presence in my room unless I command you to change, is that understood?" His voice was stern. "Obviously, you will always be naked here. This will be your position whenever I ask you to kneel. It doesn't matter whether you're here or in public, dressed or naked." Sebastian could see her conspicuous grimace at the words 'public', 'dressed or naked'. "Do you get it?" He could easily sense that she was as yet concerned about the word 'public'. It took almost a minute for Heather to understand that a question had been shot at her to answer.

"Yes." Her words sounded like a whisper. "W...will I b...be n...n...naked in p...pub...blic?" Heather's soft lips trembled as she imagined the debasement she would undergo if she were ever to do that.

"You didn't address me appropriately. Do you wish to try once again, or want me to add that as another demerit?" Sebastian gritted.

Heather shivered as her eyes widened, goosebumps were coursing all throughout her naked skin, and she breathed in sharply and blurted out, "Yes Sir. I'm sorry Sir. I acknowledge and understand this is the position I will take whenever I'm in your presence, Sir."

"Good. I'm going to consider this as a demerit since you failed to address me properly. Your punishment will be executed afterward. Remember always, you will always address me as 'Sir', and 'Sir' must be used every time you speak to me. And now for your knowledge, whether you'll be stripped in public or not, yes, you well might be." Sebastian asserted sternly.

Sebastian watched pleasingly as her mouth gaped for several seconds. Her internal struggles were intriguing to observe, he thought for a moment that she would protest, or scream her disgust. Be that as it may, at long last, Heather shut her eyes and then her mouth. She swallowed hard. Gradually she opened her eyes once more. There was a trace of tears in them, her vision was somewhat blurred, but she didn't utter a word, just blinked a few times in a desperate attempt to hold her tears back. She anxiously and eagerly waited for her Sir to speak again.

"It is time we give a quick rundown of your basic training techniques, rules, and protocols." Sebastian asserted. "I believe that you're well aware of what lies ahead. Yet next to you are the guidelines and prerequisites of your training. There is likewise an agreement, consenting to be trained, and surrendering yourself to me so that you might be trained, and consenting to any methods thereof, and use of your body for that very purpose. I need you to go through them and understand them now."

In spite of what she had experienced, and what she craved for, Heather was still alarmed to read the papers. "Do they contain things that are not meant for me or that I couldn't deal with? Will the contract bind me to him forever? Is it a consensus to do horrible things to me?" Gradually her hands maneuvered to the small pile of papers but ceased its movement at the uproarious clearing of his throat.

"You're to acknowledge every command and instruction whenever it is delivered. Your 'Yes Sir' reveals to me that you understand and consent to perform the said command." Sebastian asserted.

"Yes Sir, Sorry Sir, I will remember that in future." Heather acknowledged. When Sebastian didn't utter a word further, she grabbed the first document. It was the contract. Her eyes brushed over the lines as her mind was focused to understand the contract. The first segment needed her consent to train her as a sexual submissive and the various clauses depicting the secrecy of the process. It also included clauses consenting to her full usage like a sex slave (three orifices clearly specified) and her approval of corporal and different punishments and bondages. Heather began to perspire, and inhaled slowly, and profoundly. She clearly understood that, but seeing it engraved on a piece of paper, and realizing she would need to initial and sign, made it all the more alarming genuine. Next, it gave the trainer, Sebastian, the privilege to exhibit her to others during her training. That stopped her, and she reread the clause repeatedly just to ensure if she was reading it correctly. Heather gazed toward her master and gulped the thick lump in her throat. Gradually, her eyes returned back to the agreement.

There was a clause restricting her right to take any sort of legal actions and prosecutions against her trainer and his associates. Furthermore, another clause denying her to converse with anybody regarding her training or the identity of any of those involved in her training. There was another clause about employing her in temporary jobs, odd jobs with her handing over to him the amount earned. Heather regarded that clause to be unfair and was somewhat terrified. Clearly, she was unable to understand how her earnings from a job could be handed over to her master. Heather gradually rationalized that real slaves would work without any payments of any sort. At last, there was an attachment, her questionnaire, denoting her experience, and the level of unquenchable wants and perverted fantasies she wished to fulfill. Heather skimmed it, wondering whether Sebastian had enlisted too few rules and protocols, and had printed an excessive number of her twisted fantasies.

Sebastian's signature was already on the left. But, Heather was curious regarding the two signature lines on the right with her name printed underneath both. "Besides, why are there three copies of the agreement?" Heather wondered desperately.

She put down the document and started to wonder about the clauses.

The first few rules had already been implemented without her prior knowledge.

Strip and present quickly upon arrival in his presence.

Address Sebastian as 'Sir', and to utilize it whenever she would respond.

Furthermore, it also restricted her ability to speak, except for her responses while questioned, or pleading to speak first...

Then her eyes brushed through the new ones.

Heather was forbidden pants; just skirts or miniskirts, regardless of when or where. She could wear shorts for yard work, but only if they were acknowledged by her master, and could get permission for jeans depending on circumstances, like a dinner date. She could never wear bra and panties when she would visit him and that on specific days at any time. No bra on Mondays, and Fridays. No panties on Tuesdays, Thursdays, and Saturdays. Also, neither on Sundays, nor on any day he so wished.

Heather was required to report three days per week to his apartment for her training. The time of arrival and departure would be discussed beforehand so that they never would interfere and interrupt her daily routine and normal life. (Heather hoped that implied she could be home in time before her kids return from school or tuitions.) But other times, she would be engaged at the sole servitude to please her master. Also, she would keep him informed of her availability.

Heather would consistently thank her trainer for any attention whatsoever he gave her. Be it sexual use, punishment or whatever.

She would be given tasks, some reading, some written, some of the different other sorts. She would complete them honestly, completely and on schedule.

That Heather would be given a safeword. Be that as it may, on the off chance that she used it, some other sort of punishment might be implemented as a substitution. Moreover, if she used it pointlessly or lacked seriousness, it might be revoked for an indefinite time period. She looked upward.

Sebastian gave her a couple of minutes to digest what her mind just read. Then, he asked, "Are you ready to sign the agreement and follow all the rules and protocols mentioned herein?" Heather nodded her approval. He waited. It took a couple of more minutes before she understood what she dearly missed in her replies.

"Yes, Sir." She replied. He delicately took her chin and lifted it slowly till her eyes were locked on his.

"I won't allow you to disappoint me." Sebastian asserted.

"Move to the far end of the table and kneel. I want you to bend over the table and keep the contract before you with the pen next to it." He watched intently while she followed his orders word by word.

"Good girl. Now I want you to read the contract out loud. I want a confirmation that you will adhere to the contract in the best possible way." He continued, "You'll then ask my permission to sign it. When acknowledged, you'll initial all the spots showed and sign all the three copies on the top line as it were. When you have signed and initialed, the agreement will be consummated. Since you missed your first attempt to sign the contract because of unforeseen circumstances and reasons, rather than preparing your juicy cunt, I will lube that little puckered star in your rear end while you read the contract out loud."

Heather swallowed hard, and a little cry escaped her lips. Sebastian just gazed back at her without any emotion and proceeded. "When you've signed, you'll plead before me to use you for my pleasure. You will ask in as many ways as you can, using the most realistic terms. I won't consummate the agreement until I am overly pleased with your earnestness, and terminology. Then, during the demonstration, you will proceed, by telling me how much you need it, how much you need it completely or harder, that you are so happy to get it, and how it feels, and all these by using realistic terms. Do you get it?" Sebastian peered into her eyes, but Heather thought her sole existence was inflamed by his words.

Heather was still gazing at him. In any case, now her mouth was opened, and her eyes, once again, widened like saucers.

"Or then again, you may go out of that door, dress and never return," Sebastian stated firmly.

Her mouth snapped shut. Through his hands-on experiences, Sebastian knew that when his trainees reached this point, they in no way could deny their desperate urge for his training because not going through his training was more terrible than the fears and nervousness they all got now. He had never failed in his attempt to sign his slut contract. His psychological and structured approach included screening them too well beforehand. They were arriving at their sexual peaks. They were generally divorced or without partners. They had not been getting any, or not getting enough of their savage sexuality, and were mostly inexperienced in fulfilling their dreams. Besides, they had fantasies, twisted and perverted ones too risky to disclose to even their trusted ones. Sebastian was fascinated as he watched Heather's mental struggles battling to make the final decision, and gradually, as usual, like all his previous trainees, Heather too realized there was just one choice, a choice she had already made even before she stepped into the devil's den. He saw the standard tear form. All his trainees had undergone the same mental distress; the feeling of realizing they were trapped by their desperate wants, urges, and needs. Sebastian knew it was difficult because it was always put forth toward the end of this first session. He would enable them to talk through it, so it wouldn't emerge tomorrow, and make them miss a session, and the punishment that accompanied it. He experienced, realized and learned in a hard way during his initial days as a dominant when his early trainees missed a session or two, yet he was successful to make them return. So he helped his new trainees to pass that dilemma. Heather turned back to the pages of the agreement and began to read it out loud. Her lips trembled, the voice was hesitant initially, and Heather had to rub the tears away before she proceeded to the second paragraph.

"I, Heather Cohen, do hereby enter into a contract with the sole purpose of sexual submissive training. I, therefore, enroll in such a training course offered by Mr. Sebastian Quinn, and/or his associates. I consent to all sexual and non-sexual activities enlisted in the contract and the questionnaire to even those not enlisted herein. I do hereby consent to the penetration of any/all of my body cavities, either by Mr. Quinn, or any of his associates..."

Sebastian grabbed the tube of lube and pressed the gel out sufficiently settling it to his finger. Then, he began to massage it on the rosebud of her butt. Heather gasped terribly, but soon proceeded with her recitation. He worked another sufficient lump of the gel into her anal cavity.

"Sign it, slut," Sebastian commanded. Gradually, she grabbed the pen. She hesitated for one last time, then filled in the date, and signed the first copy. As she did, he placed his cock just at the entrance to her rectum. He felt a shiver run through the connection. He looked as she signed the other two copies and initialed all the pages. Then Heather looked over her shoulder.

"Beg for your sodomy, slut," was all Sebastian stated, as he glared back into her eyes as if daring her. "Oh my god, I haven't considered it in those terms." Heather shivered as streams of savage excitement moistened her inner thighs.

"Yes, please use my ass, Sir" Heather stated, but her voice was just a whisper. "Please, take my ass... Stick it in me, Sir." Turning back over her shoulders only to find her master not much impressed, her desperation heightened. "Fuck my ass... Fuck it with that big cock. Yes, you own it. Oh, you're tearing my ass apart, oh fuck," Heather was getting edgy to get it over with. "Fuck my ass hard, Sir. Show me who owns this ass. Please, ream out my butt hole, Sir. Please give it to me, Sir. Fuck your slut hard, Sir." The words were starting to have an impact. Her breathing fastened and grew erratic and it seemed that Heather meant every damn word erupting from her mouth. "Fuck me... Fuck your slut, Sir. Please put your cock in my ass. Please, don't make me wait like this...Sir, just do it...Pleeaassee. You already took my anal virginity at the shopping center. Now tame that bloody hole of your slut, Sir." Heather screamed in desperation.

Sebastian grabbed soft and muscular ass cheeks and spread them wide apart with the entire force of his hands and thrust forward marginally. A faint moan escaped her throat. When nothing else happened further, she realized she had to continue with her pleas. Heather shivered as her heart continued dancing in her throat, "Heather, if his eyes expressed his twisted love for you, if his words proved how much he desired you, then it's his hands that exhibited he owns you." A more perverted part of her mind screamed in ecstasy.

"Oh my God, Oh this is going to hurt, Sir. But please

don't stop until you have punished me hard. Just do it, Sir. Get it over with. Take my ass. Fuck it, please. Shove it in. Give your slut that cock, Sir. Teach your slut a lesson, Sir. SODOMIZE ME." Heather screamed in ecstatic delight.

He thrust in more firmly, but neither too hard nor too fast. He was in absolute control.

"Oh my god... It hurts. Shit that hurts bad... So big... Your cock is so big. My ass feels so full...Ohhhh...You make me so full. Fuck your slut's ass, Sir." Heather was flying the zeniths of passionate euphoria. She belonged to him. In her mind and in her body, she yearned for him. As his presence ran through her, she got addicted to him.

Sebastian was completely in now; he gave her a couple of moments to adjust to her anal invasion.

"Oh my god...So big...Your cock is so big...So full. That hurts...Please take it out, Sir."

So he did, he gradually pulled back. But not that entire hardened erection; he just let the bulbous cock head rim her anal cavity. Then he thrust back in, little forcibly than before.

"Oh! Oh god...Eeehhh... you're in my ass...you're going to fuck this slut... So, just do it...Fuck your slut's ass,

Sir. Please do it, Sir...Fuck your slut like I mean to be."

So he did. Sebastian began a rhythmic and slow back and forth pace. Then when Heather didn't utter a word a few seconds, he spanked her ass cheeks imprinting his fingers on it, and scolded her, "Scream you dirty slut. Speak up what you want. Tell me what you need. Tell me how it feels to have your first slut fuck, up in your ass."

"Oh my f... god...it still hurts, Sir...Fuck my ass...I feel so full of your big cock...It feels so enormous back there...Please fuck that butt hole. It's so depraved. Fuck your slut harder, Sir. Shove that big cock in deep...Fill me with your cock...Please, Sir...give me your cum...Bugger your slut."

The impact of relentless begging, of commenting continuously on her anal invasion, was having its powerful, stimulating impact. Her pussy was trickling, Heather realized. She was getting so aroused. That aggravated it, and better when she understood this. She would and could never be the same girl she once used to be. His intensity had marked her forever, changer her forever. Her days with him would thrill her. Her days without him were going to haunt her. She had to hold fast to her restless heart as he had transformed her forever.

"Oh, this is so humiliating. But fuck my ass. Take it. Claim it. Own it. I love to be ass-fucked. This feels so embarrassing, but so good." Heather gasped.

"Tell me how much you like this slut. Tell me how much you've yearned for this. Tell me to cum in your ass deep, slut." Sebastian exclaimed. Heather realized she couldn't withstand any further to this kind of treatment. This and that's only the tip of the iceberg. That, alongside pummeling in her ass, being compelled to verbalize, was heating her buried savage lust to the boiling point. She could feel it now. Her nipples were hard and erect like stone chips on her squashed bosom, threatening to lift her off the table. Her clit hard and throbbing, like the times during her best masturbation, her amorous adventures with this same man in the mall, and there was yet so much more to come. Also, her mind. Every one of these things and the sensations from her rear end was persuading her that this was what she had itched from the beginning of her puberty.

"Yes, Sir. Fuck my ass hard... Stick your big cock in hard. Slam it hard. Sodomize me, Sir. Cum in my ass! Make...Me...your...bitch."

Sebastian was reaching the zeniths of his excitement. With those words, he reached around and stroked her pulsating clit. The words stopped. But not the muscles in her throat, not her voice. Groans stopped. They turned out to be delicate screeches that finally were involuntarily cut off.

Heather peaked her excitement. A tremendous, consuming and overwhelming climax soon followed. Her back arched, and her body got stiff. As her ass cheeks gripped him tightly, Sebastian tribute his offering into her anal cavity.

"That's insanely awesome," Heather wondered. She was experiencing one of her best ever climaxes. FROM BEING ASS FUCKED. As the climax receded, the embarrassment of this idea sent her into an extra tremor of uncontrollable and overpowering desire.

While still in her, Sebastian leaned down and murmured in her ear, "Well done, slut. I'm happy you lived it up. He slipped from her, as she rested, gasped hard to catch her breath. Sebastian then used a soft fabric to clean them both.

"Oh my god," Heather wondered as her master's words continued reverberating in her mind. "I am a slut. I asked for it. And, I liked it." Tears filled her eyes. Hardly did she realize that her tears were releases of ecstatic bliss. But Heather regarded them as tears of disgrace, which just caused her more humiliation; her cheeks reddened and burned. More tears streamed down her eyes.

After long moments of pain and pleasure, her tears had stopped. But she was still lying on the floor in her embarrassment completely exhausted. Be that as it may, all of a sudden, there was a pair of legs before her. Her master's legs. Sebastian bowed on one knee and delicately lifted her chin till her eyes met his.

"Don't misunderstand the tears. There is nothing to be embarrassed about experiencing sexuality. You have opened the gates to your sexuality. It is a sensational and overwhelming thing." Sebastian leaned down further and kissed her brow.

Heather couldn't believe the fluctuated emotions that gentle kiss stimulated in her. When she saw her reflection in his expressive retina, her mind screamed, "Heather, there's nothing more intimate than seeing your own reflection in his eyes. You know this is where you belong." She shivered as goosebumps coursed through her skin. She realized that she had never yearned to be safe. She always craved to lose herself in the presence of a dominant man.

Taking her arm, he helped her from the floor and made her sit on a footstool. Then he got her a glass of water. She polished off the glass in one gulp, and he gave her another. "Whenever you're in my presence, I'll whisper the naughtiest and dirtiest fantasies in your ear and you'll crave to fulfill them," Sebastian whispered in her ear.

Then, when she was revived and had calmed, Sebastian asserted, "The time for your slut training has arrived."

Sebastian initiated her training on different submissive positions.

Kneel, Heather was already aware of that, but its Lifestyle name was Nadu and she had just known that. Moreover, he ensured her improvement in her previously held position. With her head held high, eyes down, knees spread wide apart to the point of straining, shoulders and back marginally arched thrusting her juicy udders outward, and Heather was a gifted learner to become a perfect sex slave. "I might have missed my luck if she was my good employee in the shopping mall." Sebastian wondered. Finally, her hands rested on her thighs with palms pointing upward.

He made her reiterate the position name, and acknowledge it before educating her on her next submissive position.

Bracelets: a submissive position which involved placing the hands behind the back, shoulders, and back arched back, thrusting her succulent bosoms outward, the fingers of one hand firmly grabbing the other wrist behind the back, a perfect position to be bound or restrained. Sebastian made Heather reiterate the position name as if he was educating a child. Then, he commanded, "Kneel". She assumed her Nadu position without a delay. "Bracelets," he commanded next. And Heather assumed her position once again. "Looks like you're quite eager to learn, slut. That's good," Sebastian chuckled deviously.

Crawl: Heather assumed her submissive position on all her four limbs, palms spread on the floor, and ass pushed high up.

"Crawl," Heather reiterated and crawled on the floor in a little circle like a puppy. "Nadu, bracelets," Sebastian directed and she followed and demonstrated. "Nadu, crawl," Sebastian smile widened when his brilliant student enthusiastically demonstrated the moves.

Table: Heather was down on all fours, her elbows locked, hands straightened, making a smooth, level on her back, her head held up straight with the level of her back. This was a position where she might be used a footrest, a human table to serve drinks and snacks. Once again, she rehashed the procedure, and then all the submissive positions she had just learned.

Karta or Slaver's Kiss: Kneeling on the floor and thighs

spread apart, which enabled Heather to touch the floor with her chest. Leaning forward, she had to place her ample bosoms and forehead against the floor. She reached out with her arms completely extended, palms against the floor. Exposing her rear end completely, she was anticipating the caress of the leather paddle or her master's cock penetration. She reiterated the name of this position and assumed the position with a shiver as she felt the vulnerability and helplessness of this position. Then again, Sebastian made her go through the full list of positions.

SULA-Ki or Slut Position: Heather lay on her back, hands stretched wide apart on both sides, palms facing upward. Her legs were spread wide open and hips up off the floor. This position resembled beckoning with her body, encouraging her master's assessment or sexual use. Once more, she trembled in this position, regardless of whether in dread or expectation, she didn't know.

Sebastian made her rehearse the position several times until she had imprinted them vividly in her mind without any further instructions from him on assuming the position correctly. He even mixed up the positions to check his slut student's attention. Heather rehearsed for about 30 minutes until she was absolutely drained and her master got bored with the monotonous play.

Finally, when it was over, Sebastian let Heather sit and relax, helping her to rejuvenate with snacks and water.

Then he took two heavy copper wrist bracelets, asked for his slut student's right hand, clasped it and repeated the same on her left hand. Then, he used a chain to bind the bracelets with one another. Grabbing the chain, he lifted her hands and encouraged her to get on her feet. Then, wasting no further time, Sebastian led Heather into his kitchen; a typical one like the ones of any bachelor. With unclean dishes in the sink, the stove and patio messy, it really needed a desperate cleansing.

"Get to work, slave." Sebastian stated, "This is your punishment for missing your first appointment," and then he left. Heather started to take care of the messy kitchen; cleaned the dishes in the sink, washed and dried the dishes, and placed them properly in the rack. She strived hard in her assignment as the restrictions of the chains tied to the bracelets made it more difficult to move her wrists freely. Then, she cleaned the patio and scrubbed the kitchen floor, mindful that it took every last bit of her body because she needed to move both hands together. Eventually, she had to lean, twist, and bend in every possible way, transforming her cleansing assignment into an exhausting and unpleasant ordeal. Although the brush and dustpan tried their best to help her, as time proceeded, she was severely depleted. She needed to move her delicate knees, and coordinate both hands to facilitate the sweeping motion, and after that with the snubbing of her wrist, figure out how to clear things into the dustpan. When she started to consider her tasks, she found it was extremely mortifying. Additionally, she faced a serious, advancing interruption. Ever since cleaning the dishes with running water, Heather experienced a developing urge to clear her bladder. When she had finally completed her kitchen assignment, her urge was too terrible to resist.

Heather returned to the living room where her master was reading. He didn't even gaze upward, so she stood before him. When minutes passed on without any responses from him, her bladder was filled up to the point of blasting in her stomach, and then Heather realized that she had to assume 'Nadu' position. Without any further delay, she slowly spread her legs wide and knelt. She waited another couple of minutes, and it was impossible for her to remain still. Her toes arched inward. Finally, when Heather could stand it no more, and a faint groan got escaped her lips.

Sebastian had been watching his slut's torment discreetly from the corner of his eyes. "What is there about a woman in an urgent and desperate need of using the toilet that is so sexually arousing?" He wondered and watched her closely for another minute;

she was practically dancing on her knees. Sebastian chuckled at his slut's painful ordeal.

Finally, Sebastian rose from his seat and grabbed her right hand. Heather was desperate for a release as the pressure in her bladder had risen considerably and her left hand reached to her crotch; Sebastian pulled her to the washroom. He stood at the doorstep. Heather hesitated, but he nodded his approval. She delayed just a few seconds and raced to the commode. As she sat, his eyes got locked on hers for a moment; Heather desperately prayed her master would look away. But when she realized the inevitable, she blushed and turned away. And as the stream began, her cheeks burned with humiliation, as the stream gained pace the deeper was her embarrassment. It wasn't the first time her master had watched her pee. But no matter what, she would always consider it demeaning by all extents. She felt mortified, exposed, and powerless. The relaxation of pressure in her bowels made her intensely relieved, but the idea that another man had watched her excreting made her reddened. Heather finished, cleansed herself dry, and then stood. She saw her master cross the doorstep, and pushed her to her knees adjacent to the commode. Then, he stood before it.

"You may help me now." Sebastian chuckled.

"Help him? How? Oh crap. He wants me to... To take out his cock... And hold it; point it to the sink while he's peeing. This is too much," Heather felt her eyes getting teary, her skin and cheeks burning under his fierce gaze and her heart pounding like bass drums. She hadn't considered it yet. Today, she hadn't even touched it with her hands or lips and now when she had to do it; it had to be for such a base reason. Gradually, Heather lifted her hands, trying to use them on his zipper. Slowly she lowered the zip down and snaked her long and lanky fingers inside. She grabbed his cock. She had already realized it was enormous as she had tasted it on all her holes, but still, she gasped hard in amazement as her master's cock came into her sight. She took care of it as she tried to figure out how to point it with both hands. Within seconds, he shot a long stream just inches away from her face. She viewed captivated in a way at how it throbbed first, and the vibe of the stream through the more slender tissue on the underside. Then it was bouncing in her grasp once again, as he worked the last drops from his bladder. Then, within the next couple of seconds, Heather recalled overhearing male discussion, and she gave it a jerk to free it from the last residual droplets. She grabbed a bit of paper and cleaned the tip. Then when Heather was about to return the shaft to its scabbard, Sebastian stopped her.

"Take it in your mouth, slut," Sebastian commanded.

Her eyes widened and glared up. Indeed she wanted it in her mouth. She needed to please it. Taste it. But not in the washroom. Kneeling on the hard tile. With the smell of both their pee in the commode. This wasn't how she desired to please her master or want it to be. Then again, her master's wishes were her commands.

Be that as it may, gradually Heather leaned forward, and opened her mouth. She realized she needed to do what he desired. What she yearned for as well. Heather licked the tip and then proceeded a little further. Then she brought it into her mouth. As she worked it gradually into her mouth, the surroundings, the environment soon vanquished from her mind. She continued her best and gave a valiant effort as the erection gradually developed in her mouth. Then when she got it completely erect, she slipped it out and licked the entire length with her tongue. She had always enjoyed doing this for her boss back in the shopping mall and now she was enjoying it more in his home. Heather tried to take in as much as she could, no matter how enormous the erection was. She choked, salivated it, and slurped on it long before it even penetrated her throat. Still, Heather tried and soon her head was bobbing back and forth showering her oral tributes to her master's potent erection. She tried to caress his scrotum, but it was increasingly difficult to do with her restrained hands. Sebastian loved the feeling of her soft lips and warm tongue wrapping tightly around his cock. He sensed her throat going into spasm as Heather struggled the urge to gag. As he throbbed inside her pretty mouth, her eyes got teary. Heather was unable to hold any longer, so she slowly pulled out and began to suck the spit off it. She took pride as her master's cock glistened in her saliva.

Heather gave her best, but knew her talent was not up to the mark as it was on previous occasions. Perhaps, the washroom environment was causing a hindrance, or the chains on her hand were hampering her movements. But in the end, with her dedicated efforts, Sebastian's erection rewarded Heather with a mouthful of protein juice. Although she battled with her reward, she strived hard to swallow her reward, no matter how overwhelming it was. When Sebastian gestured with his eyes, Heather like an excellent slave understood her master's wishes and restored his organ to his pants after cleaning it with her tongue and lips.

In no time, he lifted her by her bound wrists, led her back to the living room and ordered, "Nadu". After discussing their current session, her feelings, feedback, and future plans, Sebastian removed the chain from the bracelets and unbound Heather's wrists. He led her to the door. Heather blushed furiously as she ventured out naked outside his doorstep, stood naked there and slipped into her clothes that lay piled on the corridor floor. Sebastian placed a quick kiss on Heather's burning cheeks, stated, "Your next session will be on the day after tomorrow" and slammed the door close.

The New Master

Penny sat drinking her cup of tea in the quaint little cafe. She kept glancing to the window, looking for the man she was waiting to meet for the first time, but all she saw was the bustling market square in this, normally, sleepy village. It was a very picturesque setting for what she hoped would be a perfect first meeting. The man she was waiting for had suggested this place and she felt her heart go out to him for his choice. The setting was perfect. He knew her so well even though they had only talked via the computer and, more recently, by telephone. Her friend had called her mad for going off to meet someone she didn't know. She actually felt a bit crazy for allowing herself to fall head over heels in love with someone she had never met in the flesh. But she just couldn't help herself, probably because the spark between them had become a raging inferno of anticipation for both of them. The man who would be her Master had professed his feelings to her, unashamedly and without embarrassment, which she found both intoxicating and refreshing in a man.

Her mind was wandering now, re-reading the mails he had sent her, more so the erotic stories he had written especially for her, the ones that had gotten under her skin and shocked her that anyone could be so intuitive about her and her fantasies. How she had been turned on by them, how guilty she had felt when compelled to masturbate while reading them, her self-induced orgasms ripping through her as she read them, over and over until she was sated. When he had telephoned her and asked her had she enjoyed playing with herself after reading the stories, she had almost died of embarrassment. But he had talked to her and explained how she should never feel guilty for enjoying her own sexuality, telling her that it was a gift, and that he was flattered and pleased that she had found his writing so erotic as to have had such an effect on her.

She was lost in her dreams now, her eyes seeing another place, a fantasy in her mind where Tony arrived and simply swept her off her feet and took her with him to his room, where he would take her and use her, free her mind, bring her exquisite pleasure and totally fulfil her. She blushed as she realised she was becoming turned on. She could feel her nipples hardening under her silk blouse, the tips gently brushing the soft material as she moved, bringing a lovely tingling sensation to her down below. Down below. With a low groan she shifted her weight in her chair as her pussy tingled, the feeling spreading through her.

"Oh my god," she thought to herself, "Get a grip on

yourself woman or you'll be ready to jump on him even if he looks like a monkey."

The thought that flashed through her mind at her joke made her smile and broke her reverie. Then she looked up with a start as she realised there was a man standing in front of her, gazing intently at her blushing face. It was him, she recognised him instantly from his picture and she knew in that moment that she really did want him as his eyes blazed with passion, boring deep into her soul and scorching her beyond salvation.

"Hello my love," his deep voice resonated inside her head rather than her hearing it. "We meet at last and I must say that your pictures and your description of yourself do you no justice at all. You are beautiful and it is a pleasure to meet you and feast my eyes upon your beauty."

Penny sat gasping like a fish out of water. His voice and his presence made her feel weak, so weak that she barely managed to stammer her reply in kind.

Tony stooped and took her hand, his lips kissing gently as he let his eyes once again bore into hers. Penny stammered again as she thanked him for the kiss and tried to compliment his gentleman-like conduct. He smiled as he sat opposite her and she melted further, feeling her earlier day dreams welling up inside her again making her whole body seem to tremble with excitement. A small part of her mind was amazed at how this man could make her feel. The rest of her simply wanted him.

He, however, seemed totally calm and in control. Inside he was churning up, his stomach doing cartwheels as his mind fought with his heart and nervous system for control of his body. As always, his mind won, his body obeyed and he brought his thoughts to bear on the beautiful creature before him. When he had approached her in the cafe he had been stunned by her beauty. Next to her he felt plain and common. But he knew he loved her and so he fought with his nerves and brought his Dominant side into the fray to conquer both his nerves and his everyday worries.

He relaxed as he enjoyed the feeling of his Dominant self taking over, almost like he was two people vying for superiority inside his mind. He could see now that she was in awe of him, her eyes gave everything away to him, like windows to her soul. He drank in her every movement, her looks, every last lovely bit of her. He could see she was turned on, her hard nipples dancing freely inside the white blouse he had asked her to wear, a feeling of pleasure running through him as he saw that she had dressed exactly as he asked her to, white silk blouse with no bra, a nice tight black skirt cut to mid thigh, black stockings and high heeled sandals. He noticed she had a black leather jacket draped over the back of her chair, the strap of her handbag just visible over it. She shivered as she realised he had noticed her aroused state. She blushed even more and this realisation, in turn, made her feel even more acutely aware of her needs and feelings.

Tony stood and walked to the counter, paid for Penny's tea and beckoned her to follow him. She slipped her jacket on against the light breeze which had sprung up to take the heat out of the afternoon, and followed John outside where he took her hand in his and led her to the pub over the road from the cafe.

"You need to relax a bit," he smiled to her. He was rewarded with a nervous laugh from his woman, and that was how he thought of her already, he was sure of it, she was his now.

"You're right," she replied, I'm ready for something stronger than tea."

With that they plunged into the dimly lit bar and ordered drinks, after which they found a cosy corner and got talking about anything and everything, the alcohol loosening their tongues and their minds as they felt themselves getting closer and closer together.

As their second drinks got low, Tony asked Penny if she would like more. She was shocked when she glanced at her watch, seeing that they had been ensconced there for nearly two hours. It had felt like minutes to her, so much had she enjoyed their conversation.

"No, I'd better not have anymore thanks," she replied to his question, "I still have to drive home."

The look in her eye as she spoke the words betrayed her feelings. She wanted nothing more than to spend the night with Tony, in fact the way she felt now she wanted to have him as her Master for the rest of her life, but the serious little part of her mind kept telling her not to be stupid, she didn't know him, they hadn't even done anything together yet, he might be useless in bed or a useless Dominant. But that voice in her mind was frozen as he once again let his eyes bore into hers as he spoke in that lovely, low tone that made her blood rush.

"You don't have to leave, I have a room booked in a local hotel. I wasn't presuming anything of you, I just didn't want to drive all the way back tonight. But now I know I would love to have you as mine, my submissive, my slut. I want to take you back and strip you naked, put you across my knee and give you your first ever spank. I want to make you fly, to give you the pleasure you deserve. I need you and want you. Will you be mine? Will you come with me and obey me?"

Penny was frozen, her mind reeling, her whole body was on fire, her skin was tingling as she let every word he had uttered replay in her mind. Strip me? Spank me? Make me his? A slut? A submissive? Flying? Pleasure? Oh god yes I'll be his she screamed in her head. But all she could manage to reply to him was to meekly nod her head and to blush a gorgeous deep crimson. The blush made Tony's blood boil inside him. He was so mad about this woman, he loved everything about her and felt that he had known her all his life and yet still knew nothing about her. A wonderful paradox. He would have to be careful she didn't drive him crazy.

Arm in arm they strolled to the hotel, nothing more than a large pub on the edge of the village but with a certain homely charm to it. With hardly a glance at the check in desk, Tony led her upstairs and to his room. Penny, for her part was glad that she was arm in arm with him because she was sure her legs would have given way without him to lean on, she felt so nervous, almost scared, but oh so excited. She could no more back out of this now than she could stop breathing. It was her desire, a need deep inside her, a need created by this man holding her, a need which was threatening to burst out of her soon as she felt so aroused. Every fibre of her being crackled with tension, every part of her feminine nature demanded that she surrender herself to Tony, to have him give her everything she had wanted to try for so long. Her mind came back to the present as she heard the key click into the lock of the door to his room, the light momentarily blinding her as Tony switched the light on and led her inside.

He took her coat and hung it up next to his own then he turned the low, bedside lamps on before switching off the brighter overhead lights.

"Make yourself at home my love," He said as he lit some scented candles on top of the drawers and the bedside units.

Penny seated herself on the edge of the bed, her legs demurely together, her hands folded self-consciously across herself. Tony stood in front of her, extending his hand to her. She took it as her eyes gazed up at his, almost pleading. She knew she wanted everything he had told her would happen, but she was scared now, more afraid of her own reaction than anything else. Tony pulled her up from the bed, gently turning her from him so she was stood in front of him but with her back to him. His arms came around her, hugging her close.

It felt so good for both of them, so right. Her head turned, her face leaning up to him, beseeching him. He leaned in closer and reached down, his lips crushing hers as he kissed her, gently at first, but then with a ferocity and passion that shattered her self control and silenced the little voice in the back of her mind. She loved Tony, of that there was no doubt, but oh god how she wanted him as well, needed him to just throw her naked on the bed and use her. As her thoughts were rampaging through her mind though, Tony broke the kiss and told her to stand straight. Her mind didn't register his order immediately, but when he growled it into her ear she found herself stood to attention and waiting his pleasure.

His hands were in her blonde hair, savouring every touch of the long tresses flowing over his fingers. Ripples of delight danced up and down her spine at his touch, her shoulders twitching with the pleasure of it all. Then she felt something else and before she knew it she was blindfolded, her hands reaching up instinctively to remove it until his hands took control and stopped her.

"You will not touch the blindfold at all my girl," he whispered to her, his mouth against her ear, his lips darting soft kisses onto her neck and ear lobes, making her shiver more.

She obeyed and from that moment was his submissive, her obedience sealing their pact. His hands stroked softly over the silk of her blouse, stroking her skin through it but always stopping before they reached her nipples, those most sensitive of parts which were now crying out to be touched. But he teased her, building up her need and desire, he was in control of her now in every way. Slowly, as his hands continued their torturous way across her body, they unfastened buttons on her blouse along with the catch and zip on her skirt. Without her being aware, he was soon sliding the silk from her shoulders and completely off her, revealing her breasts with their wonderfully erect nipples to his adoring gaze. He laid the blouse over the chair and then helped her step out of her skirt which had now fallen to the floor at her feet.

Tony gasped as he drank in her beauty. Here she was, the woman of his dreams, naked and submissive to him, clad only in high heels and black lace top stockings, every inch of her skin so soft and silky, the black stockings and shoes just helping to add an air of sheer sexuality to her. He realised he was hard inside his trousers, He wanted her more than he had ever wanted anything. But his self control worked. This wasn't about him now, this was for Penny, his need becoming more to pleasure her, to free her mind and soul, to see her fly.

His concentration became immense. She couldn't see him but his face was a mask of studiousness as his every move elicited moans and whimpers of ecstasy from his slut. Yes his slut. The way she moved and begged wordlessly for his touch made her so. Her mind was fixed on his every movement on her skin. He teased her on and on as she swayed on her feet, her body burning as his touch took her higher and closer to the edge. And yet he had not touched her most sensitive parts. No matter how she moved she could not get him to touch those places she most needed him to touch. He avoided her nipples and her pussy easily, intent on teasing her further.

He left no other part of her untouched, exploring every inch of her in his quest. Her legs were shaking now so Tony guided her to sit on the edge of the bed as he raised first one of her feet, then the other, to remove her shoes and stockings. As much as he enjoyed her clad in them he now needed her naked. He pushed her back onto the bed and spread-eagled her, her body complying meekly with his demands, her mind belonging to his now. She was lost in him. His hands stroked everywhere, behind her knees as her legs raised up, the soles of her feet which made her arch her back, this movement giving him the chance to stroke her sides to greatest effect. She was supercharged now, electricity coursing through her every fibre, her body demanding that he touch her nipples, her pussy, her ass. Then his hands rolled her onto her front, his legs settling astride hers, she was dimly aware that he was naked now but not remembering when he had removed his clothes.

Then the cold oil dripped on her back, making her cry out and arch her back in agony and ecstasy. A shiver ripped up and down her back but he settled her, his hands taking control of her, pushing her down firmly on her belly as he proceeded to rub the oil into her back, his strong fingers massaging all the tension from her overwrought muscles, totally soothing away the knots which had formed during her sexual build up. On and on, the oil was smoothed into her, her back, her arms, buttocks, legs, feet. She could feel herself drifting away on waves of bliss as this man led her ever onwards.

She became vaguely aware that she was awake. Her eyes flicked open to see Tony sat next to the bed, his gaze intent upon her. She realised with some embarrassment that she must have fallen asleep as he had massaged her. She began to cringe inwardly but was halted by his smile.

"How do you feel now my darling?" he asked of her.

Penny took a minute to explore her feelings, at last coming to the conclusion that she felt absolutely wonderful. She realised she had been covered up and now she was feeling warm. Her mind was still away though, she could only watch, mesmerised as Tony approached and pulled the covers away to reveal her naked body again. He helped her up and then he sat down in the chair again. Penny stood naked in front of him as he gazed adoringly at her beautiful body with its shaven pussy and pert breasts, large dark nipples and flat stomach.

"It's time," is all he said as he gently pulled her down over his knee.

She went over him willingly and with a feeling of freedom. Here was what he had meant, true freedom, total submission to his will. Once she was settled he let his hands roam freely over her again, eliciting the same response from her, more groans and whimpers, the same thrusting of her hips as her desires grew strong and urgent once more. But his hands were now concentrating on her ass more and more. She knew her spanking was upon her and she needed it so badly. She almost laughed at the realisation that she wanted this so much, the thing she had been so nervous about.

"Spank me please Sir," she whispered as his hands carried in their gentle warming of her ass cheeks.

"I can't hear you slut," came his reply, "Say it louder."

"Spank me please Sir," she tried, her voice louder but still not loud enough for him to do as she asked.

"You'll only get what you desire when you allow

yourself to beg me for it properly. Be my slut, Beg for what you want from me."

"Oh Master, please spank me," she almost wailed, her frustration growing as his hands just kept up the stroking.

"Spank me please, Master, spank me, I'm begging you," louder now, "Pleeeaaasse, SPANK ME," a shout, her need let loose, a smile on his lips as she cried out,

"PLEASE MASTER, I'M BEGGING YOU, SPANK YOUR SLUTS ASS, SPANK ME HARD, PLEEEEEEEAAAAAASSSSEEEE."

As she cried out the last of her plea his hand came down on her. Crack, a firm stinging smack sending a lance of both pain and pleasure right through her, making her head spin with the intensity of it. Closely followed by another, and another. Every smack sending her crashing out of control, her mind reeling, lost among the stars, her body jerking, her pussy flooded and hot. And so it went on, building up, pain increasing, intense spasms racking her deep inside as her body sought its release.

Then it was upon her. The sensations were coursing through her, pain, pleasure, everything making her world spin out of control until he touched her clitoris, one fingertip lightly brushing against it, smoothing her wetness into it. And that was all it took. She shook as a massive orgasm swept through her like a brush fire before a hurricane. She cried out, she fought, but she was no match for his strength. He gathered her up in his arms and took her to his bed, spreading her out, pushing his hard cock into her spasming cunt, feeling her hands urging him into her, her legs wrapped around him, wanting every bit of him inside her urgently. She was dimly aware of a dirty minded slut begging to be fucked, to be used, to be his, and, as another wave of pleasure took her, she realised she was listening to her own voice but this time with no guilt or remorse. He gave her everything she wanted and much more, using her pleasure to feed his own needs, devouring her soul as he took her to heights she could never have imagined possible. Their passion fed them, their lust took them until they were one body, one mind, one soul, orgasm after orgasm searing them both as they tortured themselves in a blissful orgy of freedom and pleasure, both of them set free to enjoy each other and their new found love as Master and slave.

Passionate MILF Erotica by Ellie North

Ms. Clancy is an uptight lawyer who almost never breaks the rules. Since her divorce with her husband over a year ago, she's been stretched thin, attempting to divide her time among her cutthroat, demanding job, her nearly grown-up children, and rigorous yoga classes. She's had to maintain a strict schedule and be more no-nonsense than ever. But one day, her 20-year-old son Keith brings a friend over: Ben. Ben is good-looking, hot, and incredibly sexually experienced for his age. He exudes so much sex appeal that Ms. Clancy has to go to her room to let off some steam, but she's so caught up in her wandering thoughts about Ben that she forgets to close the door. Maybe Ms. Clancy will break the rules for Ben.

To say my life was hectic would be a complete and utter understatement. Between sending my kids to school, working in a competitive, cutthroat law firm, and intensive yoga classes, my schedule was constantly packed regardless of how well I attempted to organize it. It wasn't for lack of trying. I'd always been a naturally organized person, very detail-oriented and no-

nonsense. The fact that my life was falling into a mess was a bit of trouble for me.

It all reached breaking point last year when my then-husband decided we should go our separate ways. I had been furious at the time, not because I was head-over-heels in love with him or anything, but more because it meant that I now had to work even harder alone. I was used to long hours and staying up late into the night, pouring over case files and organizing evidence and sources, but having to do all that on top of being the sole caregiver to my children was another ballgame altogether.

I'll admit, perhaps a lot of it was my fault. I'd gained a few admirers after winning my last court case, some of them from within my own company, and I'd loved the attention far too much. It had made my ex-husband jealous, and my neglect of his own sexual needs over the course of that grueling case festered within him.

I suppose it was only a matter of time. My ex-husband had basically stopped showing any signs of attraction or affection towards me shortly after we'd married. Our sex life had been, at best, mundane and monotonous, like a candle that had burnt out too quickly. He'd blamed it, naturally, on my lack of adventure. Alright, I'll admit, perhaps I'm a bit of a traditionalist, but I was adventurous enough to want to play the dominant role in a few of our kinkier explorations into our limited realm of sexuality. I guess he just wasn't into being the submissive.

I jogged myself out of my thoughts. It would do me no good to think about things of a sexual nature now. I was due to pick up my teenage daughter from a birthday party in less than two hours, and I'd hardly managed to finish folding all the laundry. Too often, my mind would drift to sex, reminders of my ex-husband still hanging in the air. We'd never been great lovers, but he'd served to satisfy me sexually, and I'd been too busy over the past year to actually get laid.

I paused in front of the mirror hanging from the wall to take a look at myself. My form was lean and fit from yoga – the only exercise I still had time to do regularly – and I felt grateful for it. Maybe when I finally had time to check out the dating scene, I'd have better luck if I was in a conventionally attractive shape. I swept my blonde hair back behind an ear in an attempt to get it out of my blue-grey eyes, my full lips shooting a quick, quirky smile at the mirror. I was still in my office wear, which was, today, a tight black pencil skirt and a powder blue button-down blouse. The middle buttons were gaping slightly due to my breasts pushing through them, but it wasn't anything that couldn't be easily fixed with a safety pin. I rarely bothered changing clothes if I had to go out again later. Far too tedious for me.

I heard the front door slam shut. "Keith, are you home already?" I called out. Keith was my eldest son, and he was spending a month of his college summer break here at home before getting a part-time job. He was always bringing friends over. I didn't mind, although it was usually not the most pleasant surprise to come home from a long day of work to find a bunch of young men lounging around on my couch like they hadn't a care in the world. The only good things to come out of it were Keith having a social life, and the fact that many of his friends were pretty cute. Call me a bit of a cougar if you like, but it seemed to me that young people were getting more attractive with each generation.

"Yeah, mom," Keith called back. "Me and Ben are gonna play some music up in my room!"

"Go on then," I said, raising my voice just enough so he could hear me from the front hall. He'd been a good kid all his life, and I trusted him enough to know he wasn't lying to me or trying to sneak anything past my keen eye.

"Don't you want to introduce me properly to your mom, Keith?" another voice said.

"Come off it, Ben," Keith snapped, trying to be quieter, but I'd already heard him.

"That's a bit rude, isn't it?" I said, taking up the last of the folded laundry into my arms and striding towards the front hall. "I'll be right over for you to introduce us."

I heard Keith swear under his breath.

"Language!" I reprimanded him, finally turning into the hall.

Keith and his friend were halfway into the next room. At the sight of me, Keith sighed and stopped in his tracks, and his friend did the same.

"Mom, this is Ben," Keith said. "Ben, my mom."

"Pleasure to meet you, Mrs. Clancy," Ben said. He was taller than Keith, and he had that classic good-looking appeal to him, with his smooth features and his blazing green eyes. His hair was messy, but not too much so – just enough to give him a sexy just-got-out-of-bed look without going overboard. He was dressed alright, too. There was none of those awful cargo shorts I always tried to make Keith throw away. He was wearing jeans and a well-fitting collared shirt, and I could see the muscles in his arm rippling as he reached out to shake my hand.

"Ms. Clancy, not Mrs., please," I replied, shaking his hand. It was far bigger than mine and his grip was firm, not limp like I usually expected from my son's friends.

"Sorry! Ms. Clancy, hi," Ben corrected himself. I caught

his eyes quickly travelling up and down my frame, as though he was checking me out. But was het? His gaze met mine and I detected some desire there. I have no idea why, but at the time, seeing that look in his eyes excited me.

"Off you go, then," I said, and Keith and Ben both turned and rushed out of the room towards the stairs.

"Quit smiling," I heard Keith say in a hushed whisper and he and Ben made their way up the stairs. "This is creepy as fuck, dude, you've gotta stop this weird crush you have on my mom…"

A crush on me? The thought made me want to giggle, but at the same time, it flattered me to no end. Ben was an attractive young man who was probably quite popular with girls his age, and he had a crush on me. For some reason, thinking of that hungry gaze he'd had as he glanced me up and down and then smiled apologetically with those light emerald eyes of his was doing funny things to my stomach. The hot rush I'd felt earlier was now returning in waves. And what was really turning me on, more than anything, was the attention.

I got up to my room, where I intended on putting away the last of the already folded clothes I'd laundered, but found myself dumping the clothes on top of my dresser and collapsing into bed instead. My skirt hiked up around my thighs, too tight in my spread-out position, so I raised the fabric up around my waist. Exhaustion from the day was coming over me, but thoughts of a short nap before picking up my daughter were interrupted by thoughts of Ben. He really was something, that boy. He didn't look or act much like many of Keith's other friends, and he was far, far more handsome.

Unconsciously, I felt my hand beginning to trail downwards over my body. My fingers skirted delicately over the top of my blouse before deftly undoing a trail of buttons. My left hand slipped in then and ran over my right breast through the bra beneath, gently squeezing and molding the flesh there. I closed my eyes and hummed delightedly, enjoying the small pleasurable sensation that trickled down my spine. My left hand moved downwards, over the lightly rumpled texture of my skirt, still tucked over my waist, and then onto the softer flesh below. My fingers massaged the skin through my black lace panties, and the friction made soft moans leave my lips. My mind began to drift, wandering over to Ben, imagining what was underneath the red, collared shirt he wore, thinking of the way his back muscles might be constructed, or even better, what might be hiding underneath his jeans. At the thought of seeing Ben's cock, a rush of wetness flooded my underwear, and I moaned again, louder this time.

There was a sudden gasp from the doorway, and I realized that I'd forgotten to close my door. I hurriedly sat up, but I didn't possess enough limbs to prop myself up, pull down my skirt, and refasten all the buttons on my blouse at the same time. For a moment of horror, I wondered what Keith would do and how disgusted he would be by my state, although I'd probably give him a lesson on female sexuality to embarrass him if he said anything nasty. But, to my surprise, it wasn't Keith who had stumbled across my ajar door. It was Ben.

Seeing that I'd noticed him, Ben's green eyes widened and he ran a hand through his black hair nervously. "I'm so sorry, Ms. Clancy, Keith went out to buy batteries for his guitar and I was just bored so I wandered around." He began to back away, but not before I noticed the slight tent in his jeans. I subconsciously licked my lips. It was of very, very promising size, and seeing how flustered Ben looked made it even better.

I don't know what possessed me. I'd always been the type of person to follow the rules. Doing anything even remotely sexual with one of my son's friends who was probably two times younger than me? That was not following the rules.

But then I found myself speaking. "Come in," I said.

Ben started, surprised at being asked to come in further. "What?" he asked blankly.

"I said, come in," I repeated, and, as invitation, leaned back on my arms and spread my legs open. I knew, from his angle, that I probably looked like something straight out of a porno – hair messed up, makeup still on, blouse unbuttoned, body open and inviting. If he rejected me now, or worse, ran off screaming, this would definitely measure up to something very embarrassing. But a part of me just knew that he couldn't possibly refuse.

I was right. Ben approached me, brisk but not too eager, cautious but confident, hungry but respectful. I loved it.

"Close the door and come closer," I ordered.

Ben gently clicked the door shut, then walked forward. He came to a stop in front of me, at the foot of my bed. I waited, tense. I wanted him to make the first move, even if it meant awkwardly lying here for an hour.

It took several seconds for Ben to register that I wasn't going to say or do anything more. His gaze, suddenly hot and fevered, flicked upwards to lock with my own, and I had to bite my lip to stifle a moan at the sight of his arousal. Slowly, he lowered himself until he had sank to his knees in front of the bed, his face level with my sex. Then, without a moment's pause, he moved forward and buried his nose in my lace panties. I let out an exclamation of surprise as he inhaled deeply, taking in my scent. His groan as he exhaled was enough to make me even wetter than I already had been earlier. His hands came up to rest on either of my thighs, and at his touch, something red hot and fiery began thrumming in my veins, travelling throughout my nervous system and making me shiver.

Ben pushed my underwear aside, inhaling deeply again, and then he pressed his tongue flat against my cunt. I exhaled sharply, arching my back. His tongue was warm and wet and strong as it flicked my clit expertly, drawing circles around it and on it in a smooth, consistent motion. I reached down to fist his hair in my hands, and it felt simultaneously rough and soft. Encouraged, he latched his mouth around my clit and sucked, the pressure pulling me into a chasm of pleasure as I screamed. His mouth formed a suction around my clit at his tongue continued to work and flit against me, it was all too much, my orgasm building up steadily inside me, waiting to crash over me like a wave, and then...

Ben pulled back, grinning cheekily up at me. I moaned at the loss.

"You taste amazing, Ms. Clancy," he said, and I caught an almost dangerous sparkle in his eye. This boy was experienced for his age, and he knew it.

"Then why did you fucking stop?" I asked, bucking my hips in a desperate and fruitless attempt to get his tongue back where I wanted it.

Ben grinned again, then in one slow twisting movement, he buried his tongue deep inside me.

All I could do was scream. He was practically fucking me with his tongue, setting a pace so torturously slow I was nearly sobbing. I could feel myself getting wetter and wetter, and I could hear the sounds of my apparent arousal as Ben stretched and curled his tongue within me, working diligently, his ministrations reducing me to nothing more than a pleasured mess. I could even smell my arousal in the air, and it brought a flush to my cheeks how blatantly turned on I was.

Ben pulled his tongue out and, before I even registered that there had been a change, he replaced it with one thick finger. It slid into me with ease and instantly curled to find my G-spot, rubbing rhythmically. I could feel each movement against my walls, and then he was sliding another finger in so easily; I was so fucking wet I was surprised I wasn't completely drenching the sheets.

Ben began to move his body upwards, his fingers continuing their dance as he did so. I could feel the warmth radiating off his still fully-clothed body, could see his back rippling as he came upwards until his face was level with mine. I could see that his pupils were blown wide, lust emanating off of them in coursing waves that I was sure rivalled my own.

Ben lowered himself downwards and caught my lips in a hard, rough kiss. It wasn't romantic. Only pure passion and desperation fueled him, and the feeling was certainly mutual. His mouth was hot and his breath tasted so good and his lips were so soft and oh! I could hardly contain myself from kissing back with equal vigor. His fingers were still moving inside me, and my hips were moving in time with his fingers. Ben deserted my lips and moved down to my neck, where he licked and sucked and kissed a column up and down my throat. High-pitched, keening noises were practically falling out of my mouth by now, and my fists were tangling in the sheets, pulling so hard they might rip. How could I be enjoying this? This was my son's friend. Why was I letting him do this?

And then Ben slipped in a third finger and his thumb found my clit, and all doubts and misgivings I had vanished into thin air. It's slightly tight and the stretch stings a bit at first, but his thumb rubbing my clit sends a fresh wave of wetness over his fingers, reducing the resistance. He was pressing insistently against the little bundle of nerves in my cunt, applying just the perfect amount of pressure and the friction was just so delicious that I couldn't stop myself from squirming underneath him. I was so close, so close, just almost there…

Ben bit down on my neck, hard, and the pain shot through my body and mixed in seamlessly with the pleasure. I saw stars, and the next thing I knew, my entire body was shuddering and shaking and I was coming.

I came down from my high, panting and gasping for breath like I'd just run a marathon. There was definitely a mark on my shoulder by now, but for some reason knowing this only made my arousal begin to climb again. I'd never been the type to enjoy pain in the bedroom – unless I was the one inflicting it – but this was something else.

Ben was looming over me, unbuttoning the rest of the fastenings on my blouse and pushing it off my shoulders. His fingers, damp from my own wetness, felt warm, and his touch was sending off sparks throughout my oversensitive skin. Now that my climax had passed, I found myself wondering, once more, what the hell I was doing with this young man, but he was pulling me up into a sitting position to slide my shirt off my body, and he looked so amazed by what he saw that even a stiff lady like me had to melt.

I wrapped my arms around his neck and began to nip at his ear, his jaw line, his neck. He reached back to undo my bra, and the clasp came off easily in his hands.

Something snapped inside me and I practically growled, leaning forward and trying to pull his shirt above his head. He allowed me to do so, revealing his toned stomach and a long stretch of gorgeous, tanned skin that I immediately felt the urge to run my hands over. Ben rid me of my bra, and then his hands were everywhere on my own body as well. Still looming over me on his knees while I sat, he groped and touched parts of me that I hadn't even realized were erogenous zones – the center of my back along my spine, the curves under my breasts, the dip in the back of my spine, the soft inside of my arm. His fingers travelled like they wanted to memorize the entire terrain of me, and by god, was he memorizing thoroughly.

I couldn't take it anymore. I had to see all of him. I reached forward to undo the button on his jeans, tugging down the zip in an almost fevered rush. He helped me pull them down to his waist and kicked them off hurriedly, leaving him in only his boxer briefs. The outline of his cock was prominent through the fabric, big and hard. I latched my mouth around it and breathed in deeply, a strong scent of musk and earthiness enveloping my senses. Above me, Ben groaned softly, rocking his hips forward. I eagerly began to mouth at his cock through his boxer briefs, his reaction eliciting a delicious feeling. His cock is straining against its confines, threatening to pop out. I felt the sudden need to get my mouth around it entirely, drag my tongue along its length, suck it with all my might, lick the tip and taste the precum that must have been dripping out my now. I tugged down his underwear, revealing a thick, hard cock that was certainly much bigger than my ex-husband's.

I took Ben's cock in my hand, fascinated by how dwarfed my fingers appeared in comparison. Ben hissed sharply as I began to stroke it experimentally, feeling its weight in my hand, focusing on angles and movements that elicited the most noises from him. The heady scent of his cock was filling my head, making it difficult for me to focus, and the desire to taste him became just too much to control. With that, I wrapped my lips around the head of his cock.

The corresponding jerk of Ben's hips made my hands rush to his sides to steady him. Patience, I wanted to tell him, but my mouth was full of cock, and my god, it tasted so good. I hadn't realized how much I'd missed this, missed the taste of a man flooding my tongue.

Ben's hands were caressing my hair as I began to bob my head up and down, pausing every now and then to lick the head of his cock. My tongue wrapped around his cock in a twisting motion and I hollowed my cheeks, trying to take in as much of him as I could. Ben's response was nothing short of enthusiastic, his hips moving forwards and backwards until he was just fucking my mouth. My jaw began to ache, but it ached so good that I couldn't stop even if I wanted to. If this had been my ex-husband, I would have stopped ages ago, but Ben fueled something within me that just wanted to be dirty and used. I could feel my pussy dripping again, turned on and begging to be touched as though I hadn't just come like a freight train.

Ben suddenly stilled, then pulled his cock out of my mouth. I looked up at him, but didn't get a chance to see what was wrong before he had pushed me onto my back. He made quick work of my skirt and ripped my panty clean off of me – an act I would have surely been furious about had it been anyone else – and positioned himself at the entrance to my pussy. He rubbed his saliva-slick cock against my clit, and before this I could have never possibly imagined that an action like that could send fire shooting through my system or send any wetness flooding out of me. Still merely grinding against me, Ben leaned down and took one of my nipples into his mouth while one of his hands reached up to play with the other one. I keened, my back arching as I tried to get more of him on me. My nipples, already stiff, became even harder with his careful movements, and when he grazed his teeth along a nipple, my pussy began to want nothing more than for the cock rubbing against it to be inside.

"Ben," I moaned. "Put it in."

Ben shot me a charming grin, continuing to tease me by slowing his pace.

"Ben," I gasped. My cunt was pretty much throbbing with need by now. "I want you in me, now."

Ben was still smiling. "Ask nicely," he said.

My body's initial reaction was to be shocked. A boy my son's age was asking me to beg for his cock. That wasn't going to happen. I might have broken a major rule by having sexual relations with Ben, but I still had some dignity.

At the sight of my scowl, Ben shrugged and continued to drag his cock slowly against me. It was so fucking evil of him and I wanted him more than ever now.

"Ben," I said.

Ben ignored me, returning his attention to my breast. He molded and pinched my nipples calculatedly, measuring me responses to draw me closer and closer to desperation.

"Ben!" I cried.

Ben placed the head of his cock at the entrance to my pussy, and my heart began to race. Finally, finally, finally... But he wasn't moving. He was just staying there, waiting. I wrapped my legs around his waist and tried to pull him in, but he stayed still.

"You know the magic words," he teased.

"Come on!" I gasped, trying in vain to wiggle down onto his cock.

"Beg for it," Ben said.

I shook my head.

"Beg for it."

I shook my head again.

Ben pushed the head of his cock in a fraction of an inch, then pulled it out again immediately.

I snapped.

"Fuck! Please, Ben, please, please fuck me, please..."

That was all I had to say, and suddenly Ben slammed into me, his cock entering me at a brutal speed. I screamed, my entire body filled with spasms of pleasure. His cock felt huge inside me, stretching me out in a manner that might have been painful if not for the natural lubrication coating both his shaft and my insides. I could feel every inch of him filling me up, each stroke against my walls, each powerful thrust making me quake inside and out. It was as though the world around me ceased to exist.

I clutched at Ben's shoulders and clenched around him, reveling in his faint "Oh!" of surprise. My heels dug into his ass, legs squeezing him tighter as I attempted to get him in even deeper, my hunger and desire for him increasing and becoming insatiable. In response, he shifted slightly, and the new angle was absolutely divine.

I gave a wordless cry, now unable to do anything but cling on for dear life. He was thrusting faster and harder in that powerful way that comes with youth, battering my G-spot with every movement. I began to scream and beg, my words a tangled mess of nonsense "moreyespleasefuck", my entire body demanding more even though I wasn't sure if I could take it. Ben's hips snapped repeatedly against mine, and the friction was so delicious that I started chanting his name.

"Ben, Ben, Ben," I mewled, but that only egged him on more, making him ram into me faster and faster. His rhythm was beginning to slip, his motions becoming more ragged, but he was still going harder, somehow, and it was becoming far too much far too soon, and then –

"Fuck, Ben, I'm –" But I didn't get to finish my sentence, because the next moment, my entire body tensed as wave upon wave of pleasure crashed over me like a storm. I barely registered Ben's low moan before he pulled out of me and came all over my stomach and chest, pearly white cum coating my breasts.

Ben rolled off and collapsed next to me. It had all happened so fast.

"Next time, we should go much slower," I said, without thinking, as we lay there panting. It was only a few seconds later, when Ben replied, that I realized what I'd said.

"So there will be a next time?" he asked.

I narrowed my eyes, peering at him inquisitively, as though I was sizing him up and considering everything. In my head, though, I already knew the answer.

"Only if we keep this a secret from Keith," I replied.

Ben laughed. "Of course, Ms. Clancy."

A voice could be heard from outside my closed door.

"Ben? Dude, where are you?" Speak of the devil.

"You'd better get going," I said.

Ben nodded, getting up and quickly getting dressed before rushing towards the door. Just before he opened it, he turned around and shot me a little wink. And then he was out of my room, door slamming behind him, and gone.

My head fell back against my pillow and I closed my eyes. What I'd gotten myself into, I didn't know. But I was certainly looking forward to finding out.

In the New Townhouse

Lisa was all alone in her new townhouse in Venezia, she is pretty new in the country as a whole, her two girls had gone to their father's home for the weekend, and her husband was out with a few of his friends on a "guys-only" outing. Much of her wishes she had gone along with him because when they went away, the guys just seemed to have an excellent time-playing card, partying, flirting and gambling. He would have taken her if she had asked, and they'd have fun because Lisa enjoyed playing poker, drinking, flirting with his buddies, and gambling— heck she'd even enjoy getting a lap dance from the striper that'd probably show up somewhere over the weekend. Yet, this time, she didn't ask, not. Since she had a night alone it had been a while, so she decided to relax and enjoy every minute of it. When she stood in the kitchen making vodka and diet soda her preferred cocktail, she decided to retire to her bedroom and take a shower. The excitement of a lengthy masturbating session was a grin on her lips.

He pictured the things he would do to her as he parked his car a few blocks away, and waited. She was gorgeous and sexy and he just couldn't bear to get his fingers on her. From the first time they met, he had not been able to get her out of his head and he felt a tug in his crotch in anticipation of what he was about to do.

She took off her clothing and looked in the mirror. She was 37 years old not bad. She looked undoubtedly younger, and was often complimented by people on her beauty. Her long, light-red hair was her best feature, though she had been told she also had beautiful blue eyes. Her body was not wrong either, not too thin, not too big with large breasts and butt to snatch (or spank). Lisa climbed into the hot shower and let her body spray water. Her nipples grew instinctively taught by the experience, and as she washed her hair she was watching the shampoo bubbles run down her arms. She loved the way they looked down as the water ran down her breasts. She took the scissors to tidy up her cunt hair for a few minutes. She liked to be shaven smooth with only a small strip of hair. It was more for the look than anything else, her red hair was so bright down there it was just barely visible. She thought for a moment about masturbating with the detachable water massager, then decided to skip that for one of her other toys.

The "guys-only" travel had worked nicely for him, and he was planning to make good use of it. He had given considerable thought to what he was going to do with her when they were alone. He reached down his hand to his cock and gave it a pull as he began to grow hard.

She put on her pale yellow silk robe after getting out of the tub and drying off, then took her drink into the bedroom. She retrieved her favorite toy from the wardrobe hiding place, sliding her robe off her shoulders and down onto the floor. Lisa laid down on the bed and with a smile she reached into her robe with her hand and started to taunt the region around her breast— the skin was taut again with tiny bumps rising around her nipple. The nipples themselves were exhilaratingly huge. She slowly slid down her fingertips over her flat stomach before they pulled on her pussy fur. She picked the toy up from the bed with her other hand. She played around her clit for a couple of minutes, watching the ache intensify until she was no longer able to stand it. Slowly she slid the vibrator's head inside her cunt. Definitely, she was wet enough to take anything. She slipped it in with the next move- filling out her cunt. She could feel the vibrating contact on her clit while the shaft was inwardly pleasing her. She knew it would take her only a couple of strokes to cum; the sensations were too intense for her to last much longer. The spasms came hard and fast, and she realized with regret that what she really wanted was a real cock as she drifted off to sleep.

It all seemed to him to be too convenient. Hours after the lights had gone out, he waited in the dark outside her house. A couple of pushes and the lock emerged on the glass sliding door allowing him to reach the basement. He slowly worked his way back the staircase to the main floor with the backpack he'd brought. He took a moment to search the lock at the front door and then went to stairs for the second flight. He walked softly into the bedroom where she lay unconscious. He watched her enjoy her naked body and full breasts for some moments. He quickly stripped off his clothing and opened his pocket to cut the chains and blindfold that he had carried with him. He wrapped the rope softly around one wrist with great care, and then the other, pulling slowly until her arms rose over her head. He tied the rope to the headboard so she couldn't raise her limbs or touch him with her hands. He then slipped the blindfold over her eyes and back of her head. He stood beside the top of the bed, looking at her breasts ready to harden her nipples. He stroked his hard dick with one hand, while wetting his mouth pre-cum. Leaning cautiously over the pillow, a drop comes onto her face. He sees her slipping into her mouth as it slips over her bottom lip. He continues stoking up his arousal, bending over this time so that the slip lands on her breast. The pre-cum slowly slides down and the movement makes her nipple rigid beneath her breast. Smiling, he is heading to the other side of the bed and preparing for another drop onto her other breast. Continuing to stroke himself steadily, he moves another droplet to the end of his cock and rubs it gently over her lower lip, leaving a glistening pre-cum trail.

Lisa wasn't sure what awoke her, but noticed that her lip was tickling with something. She tastes something in her mouth as she licks her lips and when she tries to open her eyes she can see nothing. She suddenly notices her hands are bound, and her eyes are filled with something. Panic sets in as she thrashes her body on the pillow and demands to see who's there.

He says nothing while heading to the bottom of the bed and taking her leg. He takes it to the edge of the bed and wraps the second rope around it, pulling it securely under the bed and around the other side, looping the other end around her remaining ankle to keep her legs out of touch. He walks up bedside down, running his hand down her body length. He takes one of her breasts into his mouth and lets taunt it with his tongue. He can't believe he's got his hands on her, he's had many fantasies of this. He shifts over her and starts to work on the other breast.

Lisa asks him to stop at first, in terror of what is happening to her. Within a few minutes, though, she discovers that he feels very good at what he does. She decides this must be her husband, shocking her by an attack at the late night. She avoids begging and lies peacefully, allowing herself to enjoy what's going on without her leaving. She senses him moving down between her thighs after having a meal of her breasts with his hands, his moist breath just inches from her bare pussy-lips. His tongue is warm and humid as it lands on her clit, and she groans with satisfaction as this is one of the world's favorite things! He looks up with his mouth devouring her and telling her he's been waiting for a long time to taste her and he knows it's worth the wait. She just laughs, as she can hear the anticipation of her orgasm. He grips her hands as he plunges his tongue into and out of her and as she moans with ecstasy he can feel her juices flowing down his chin. He moves back up to her neck and slaps on her cheek with his dick. She turns her head toward him and in her confusion opens her mouth looking for him. For her lips, she lapses at him, enthusiastically opening her mouth, so she can get him in. He groans as his dick is enveloped by her warmth, his tongue going up and down. He squeezes her eyes shut and relishes the sensation-what a beautiful mouth she has. He takes away his dick from her and moves down to the bedside. He pulls out the chains from her feet and positions himself again between her thighs.

He wants to keep going slow. He's scared he'll cum until everything that's been arranged is over. Touching his cock to her clit, he warms her with his mouth. He pushes it slowly into her cunt, inch by inch, until she has taken him fully. For a second, he sits there enjoying his cock pulsing intruder of her. Every time, he is coming out and pressing in faster. She's warm and soft and as she passes across his shaft her lips feel like silk. He sees her hips start bucking for more, and suddenly hears her telling him to fuck her. He takes a few more strokes before he pulls back. He moves quickly to the bottom of the bed and grips her feet tightly in each hand as he turns over her body so that her knees are crossed and she's face down, he's exactly where he wants it. She lifts his head and asks him to stop. He will not. That's what he is for here. Frantically, she asks him to stop, as fear crosses her mind that after all, this might not be her husband. She starts crying out in fear about what is about to happen to her.

With both hands, he grips her ass cheeks, spreads them as far apart as possible, and shots his rock-hard dick roughly into her soft, tight ass. He can hear her screaming in agony as he always rolls in and out of her, filling her up until she couldn't possibly take any more of him. Stroke after stroke into her tight ass leaves him breathless but he can finally feel rolling her hips, rhythmically pushing her ass up to him. He pushes harder and deeper and quicker as she pleasurably calls out. Her cunt looks impressive to him and, just before he's ready to burst, he collapses on top of her sucking tightly on her neck. She hears his final moan like an animal as his cum starts to pour out of her pussy. With his own climax he can feel her shaking underneath him.

He gets off his dirty body and sets on covering himself. He takes the cord from her hands before withdrawing. When he heads down the steps he hears her yell out, "Nate, are you, right?" He walks out into the dark without responding.

Danced Around the Hall

Red, green, and yellow lights danced around the hall, leaving iridescent tinges on the people's faces who congregated inside. Everyone was mostly donned in black, holding white lights over their shoulders to give the hall a resplendent, beautiful look. On the stage before the corybantic fans, Michael Smith stood with a microphone in one hand, waving and watching as the fans mimicked him, desperate to touch him.

Michael Smith was a tall, lanky young man in his early twenties. His hair was dark, combed-back, and sleek. His trousers were sagged, revealing white, shiny underwear that matched his sneakers. Michael Smith was the lead singer of the Devil's Chariots, a collection of young men, who'd instantly hit success in Los Angeles.

Clutching onto the mic, Michael moved left, jumping up and down like a lunatic. His eyes were constricted from a high intake of morphine. He watched the few fans congregate in front of the hall replicate his moves, jumping and shouting at the top of their voices.

The band comprised seven men, and they churned out a shrill, rock music that resonated through the hall. Michael nodded, following the undulation of the guitar.

He switched the mic to his left hand, and turned his right hand, making it look like a slithering snake about to bite.

Moments later, he stooped down, arched his frame forwards and screamed. He fell down on one knee, and the iridescent lighting went off, immersing the hall in near darkness. The fans were only perceivable from the outstretched lights over their heads.

"We are the devil's chariots! Yeah! We make mischiefs that angels dread. We love your sisters and her friends. We are the devil's chariots yeahhh!!!"

Michael Smith sat down on the stage, his legs splayed east and west. He bent his face down and raised his brow up ever so slightly, revealing an eerie, crazy look. His eyes met the face of a crying lady in the audience. He blinked, trying to capture her face. Michael couldn't see her clearly. He looked away, cocking his face to the side.

"We are the devil's chariots! Yeah! We make mischiefs that angels dread. We love your sisters and her friends. We are the devil's chariots yeahhh!!!"

Michael jumped up on his feet and swiveled to the lady. Now, he could see her better. Her face was afflicted with an amalgam of joy and desperate excitement. It was easy to see that it was the excitement that made her cry. And Michael briefly thought about welcoming her to the stage, but he dropped the lid on that thought, looking away from the position of the deeply emotional lady, who seemed keen on getting closer to him.

He moved to one end of the stage, danced, then charged down to the other end. He came back to the middle of the stage, raised his hand up, drowning out the music. The lights came back on and the iridescent faces in the hall were conceivable.

Michael scanned their faces and saw the delight etched on them. He could see he'd left quite an impression on them. It was this aspect of his job that he savored.

He swiveled towards the position of the lady. Their eyes met. She was smiling amid the tears. Once again, Michael felt compelled to invite her over. Perhaps he could stretch the mic towards her and ask her a few questions. Incidentally, as he held closely to this thought, his eyes were still fixed on the lady.

Some of the fans were following his gaze, wondering who elicited such a passionate gaze from him. He smiled at her and blew a kiss. Michael felt it was enough, and he watched on as the lady caught the kiss in the air, placing it on her heart, detectably happy. The rest of the crew joined him where he stood, waving at the crowd.

Michael looked towards the position of the lady. She was no longer there.

*

Michael drove through the street of Santa Monica wearing a hoodie, and kept his eyes on the road. It was a Saturday, and the time was edging past four in the evening. A song by his band was blaring out of the speakers. He nodded to it, hurtling down the road.

The face of the emotional lady suddenly came to the forefront of his mental frame. He smiled, shaking his head pitiably. He hadn't thought about the lady since that night in Los Angeles, and it was surprising how the thought came with an instant ferocity.

He accommodated this thought with a bit of nostalgia, flipping through the pages of his memory, reliving his infallible performance on the night he met her. The ghost of a smile touched the corners of his lips. Michael could remember how he felt captivated by her appearance. How her beauty hallmarked an unmistakable, A-list, Hollywood star. She was beautiful, and perhaps if she hadn't left so early, he would've taken his time to get to know her.

As he hurtled down the road, he fastened himself

together, understanding that he'd forget her face just as he'd forgotten the many faces he'd met at different stage performances. He kept his eyes on the road, annoyed with his mind.

Michael pulled up in a grocery store, digging his hands into his pockets as he made his way down. He kept his face down, unwilling to give anyone the impression of his personality. He wheeled down a shopping cart and stocked the cart with different brands of milk and yogurts. He picked out a few bags of cereals and looked forward, apparently content with his shopping. He was making his way to the cash register when he felt a hand on his back. He turned immediately.

"Oh! Oh! I mean no harm."

Michael looked up at the face. The familiarity was striking. It was the lady he'd thought about moments ago.

"You!"

"Yeah me. I'm Samantha," she replied cheerfully.

"Are you stalking me?"

"No! No! I came to do some shopping of my own," she defended, keeping a smile on her face.

Michael examined her face, getting a closer look at her

unblemished beauty. He had the sudden idea that Samantha could make it as a model. She was certainly imbued with requisite features. He smiled at her.

"You left early that evening," Michael said.

"Oh! You remember. So you were really looking at me?" Samantha asked, excitedly.

"Of course I was looking at you. What did you think?"

"There were a lot of people. I guess I didn't think I was that special," she retorted.

"You are beautiful, Samantha. And I don't have to take a second look to notice that. And trust me. You have a rare beauty."

"Okay. You're just saying this to make me feel happy because obviously I'm your fan," she replied, locking her hands together.

"No! Sam. I'm saying this because it's the truth. You really are beautiful."

"Oh! My God. Thank you. I left early because I got a message from my dad," Samantha replied.

"Oh! How old are you?"

"Twenty," Samantha said in excitement.

"It's my pleasure to finally meet you up close," Michael

said, stretching a hand towards her.

Samantha ignored his hand and embraced him, holding tightly to him. Michael was calm, allowing her to feel his body, and she continued to hug him. She placed her face on his chest and kept it there.

"Okay, Sam. It's time to let go," Michael said, pulling away slowly.

Samantha took that emotional look again. She kept her eyes on him, watching as he rolled away from her line of vision. Her eyes had taken a wet glint, welling up with tears. Michael looked at her over his shoulder and noticed the emotion wafting from her. He stopped and turned towards her.

"Are you okay, Sam?"

Samantha nodded, and Michael could see she was close to breaking down in tears. She barely staved off the sorrow that dripped from her eyes.

"You want to take a ride with me?" he asked, with a faint smile. Her eyes dilated in disbelief.

"Yeah! Yeah!"

"Where would you want us to go?" he asked. Samantha wiped out her eyes with one hand and moved towards him.

"We could go anywhere you like. Just drive around town," she replied.

"Alright then."

*

Michael hurtled through Santa Monica keeping his eyes on Sam, who kept her face up, enjoying the music blaring out from the speakers. She knew every lyric and sang along as if she was a member of the band. Michael found himself admiring the little details about her. The way she smiled while tapping on the dashboard and nodding. The way she turned to him and smiled amorously time and time again made him smile.

Michael pulled up outside his apartment and turned to her.

"I live here," he said, smiling.

"Oh! Nice apartment."

Michael turned the ignition and sped away, taking Samantha by surprise, and chuckled as she struggled to find her balance. He stopped at a deserted park, winding down his window to take a peep at the weeds sprouting out of the broken cement floor of a basketball court.

"I used to play there," he said, turning to her.

"Seems you had quite a humble history," Samantha replied solemnly.

Michael nodded. "Someday I will tell this story better."

Michael kept his eyes fixed on the park, feeling nostalgic. He felt the hands of Samantha graze his trousers, but he pretended not to notice, keeping his gaze locked on the park.

Samantha ran her hand to his zip, and gently unzipped his trousers, then unbuckled it. Michael felt a warm rush down his belly as his dick bulged, stiffening harder as her hand slipped in. Moments later, she slowly pulled his trousers down. Once she felt his dick, she exhaled loudly, drawing it out.

She smiled as she stroked it, leaning her face to it. She dropped a thimbleful of spittle on her palms and rubbed it on the pink, round cap of his dick. She rubbed her palm on it gently, stroking, watching with delight as it continued to bulge.

Michael took his eyes off the park, dropped a perfunctory look at her, and tilted his face up, moaning gently. Samantha dribbled more saliva and stroked him before sliding the dick in her mouth. She gently moved up and down, and Michael moaned with every move, breathing fast.

Samantha pinned two fingers on the head of his dick and stuck her tongue into the tiny crevice on top. Michael's legs trembled, and he wiggled his toes in heightened pleasure. Moments later, Samantha stroked and sucked, dipping his dick deep inside her mouth, almost choking on it.

"God! You're fucking good at this. This is so good."

Michael breathed faster, feeling different rushes of fluids through his body. It had become harder for him to keep in touch with the sensual feelings through his body. He started moaning faster and faster. Samantha was sucking quickly. Stroking and sucking. She moved her head faster. Michael contracted his thighs and ejaculated. Samantha kept her lips on his dick, sucking his cum, licking happily.

"I should drive you home," Michael said.

"You don't have to. I just live down the road," Samantha replied, moving out of his car. "I had a great time," she added.

Michael watched her move down the road, take a corner, and drift away from his line of vision. He turned on the ignition and hurtled down to his apartment.

*

Michael was sitting in his living room thinking about Samantha while slurping from a glass of whiskey when he heard a knock on the door. He started towards it and opened the door. Samantha stood there with a smile on her face.

"I'm sorry. I just couldn't stop myself."

"Don't worry. Come on in," Michael replied, making way for her. He feigned a smile.

Samantha moved in, pirouetting through the apartment. She looked over her shoulder and saw Michael slouching on the sidewall, staring at her. She turned towards him, keeping an expression of unconcealed delight.

"Your place is beautiful," she said.

"Thank you. Care for a drink?"

"Yeah. You got Vodka?"

Michael nodded and moved away. Moments later, he returned with a bottle of Smirnoff Vodka and two glasses. Samantha sat on the couch when he returned. He plopped down beside her and served her.

"Thank you," she said, sneaking a sip.

Michael served himself and took down his drink in one gulp. He placed the bottle on the concrete floor and sat back. Samantha reclined, turning to him.

"So what do you love about my music?" he asked.

"Everything. The energy you put into it is obviously visible. And you look like a great guy as well. Plus you are handsome. I think you just have the right charm," Samantha said, taking another gulp.

"Do you like poetry?" Michael asked softly.

"Yeah." "Do you have a favorite poet?"

"Yeah. Robert Frost. I know he is an old poet, but I really love ..."

"Robert Frost? He's my favorite poet too," Michael cut in, interrupting her.

"Oh! That makes the two of us," she said, taking another gulp. Samantha pressed her face on the cushion, leaning closer to him.

"There's a particular stanza I really love," Michael said.

"Let me hear it."

"These woods are lovely, dark, and deep. But I have promises to keep. And miles to go before I sleep."

Samantha's eyes became terribly constricted, looking out to him amorously, looking at the movement of his lips as they uttered every word. She pressed her lips to his and kissed him. Michael kept his lip firm, reluctant to dive in. Samantha continued to press her lips to his, placing her hands on his shoulder. Michael conceded, letting her lips wade in, feeling the succulence of her soft lips. He placed his hands on her shoulder and gradually gave the kiss the attention it needed. Michael drew his lips apart and looked into her eyes.

"You want to do this?"

She nodded, keeping her eyes constricted. He held her hand and drew her up, leading her to his bedroom. He held her tight and kissed her ferociously, dipping his tongue in her mouth. Samantha held him, running her hand through his body as they kissed. He unzipped her dress, clutching her breast as it fell down from her body.

"You have a beautiful body," he said, sucking her breast. He lifted her up and dropped her on the bed. Slowly, he crawled to meet her, and Samantha arched her frame up, waiting. Michael ran his hand over her thigh, moving it to her breast.

"I'm going to fuck you so hard. Are you sure you want my dick?"

She nodded shyly. Michael took off his clothes. Samantha's eyes dilated at his fat, thick dick. His dick had become stiffened and hard. She gripped it and sucked, moving it in and out from her mouth, feeling the relentless firmness of his dick.

Michael reached out for a lubricant, and slowly rubbed it on her butt cheeks, moving his hands around her arsehole as if giving her a massage. He drifted his hands inside her arsehole, rubbing and fingering her. Samantha laid back, allowing him to have his way.

First, he dipped one finger inside her arsehole, then he stuck two in, before dipping three fingers inside, slacking the walls of her arse. He fingered her thoroughly. After a while, he held her butt cheeks apart, stuck his tongue inside and rimmed her. Samantha moaned, making soft sounds that only made his dick stiffer. Slowly, he plugged his dick in.

Moving in and out, he inserted his dick halfway in. Samantha clutched the bedspread, gripping it as he moved in and out. She bit at the foam, muffling herself up. Tears trickled down her eyes and set on the bed. Michael spanked her arse, holding her butt cheeks apart. He dipped in the full length of his dick.

"Oh! My God!" Samantha hollered.

Michael was intense now. Going in and out, fucking her as she shouted and cried.

"Is my dick as good as my music?"

"It is fucking good. God! It is good," she stuttered.

Michael turned her and placed her legs on his shoulder. Slowly, he dipped his dick back in her arse and started where he left off. This time he pressed it in, leaving the full length of his dick inside her. Samantha moaned, making a throaty, choking sound. She bit his arm, her eyes welled up with tears. Michael continued to make quick, hard thrusts, paving a smooth passage for his dick.

"Your dick is so sweet! Fuck me. Come on. Fuck me."

Michael leaned closer, pushing her waist up. He made faster movements. In, out, in, out.

"God. I can feel it in my heart."

The softness of her voice seemed to harden his dick even more. Michael was sweating now. Moving in and out, keeping her legs on his neck. He moaned, making a throaty sound.

"God! I love your fucking arse," he said, as he ejaculated.

He stuck his dick out, and Samantha pulled herself up, then gripped it. She placed the cum-ridden dick on her mouth, licking and sucking, visibly having the best time of her life.

Sloppy Time

In this case, Meredith could honestly say that she did not feel any regret for what she was doing. The ends would justify her means, whatever they may be. And she wouldn't let go of the growing excitement that urged her to keep going. How mean she felt! It would normally be easy to forgive and forget. Who's got time to spend on old grudges? But it was completely different this time. If Meredith had not stopped this now, it would never have stopped.

The situation at issue was the behaviour of Meredith's roommate, Becca. The problem of Becca was the amount of disrespect she displayed to her roommate. It could be tolerated for a short time, but it was out of the question to let it continue. This disrespect came in the form of Becca sleeping with all of Meredith's ex-lovers after they had broken up.

Now Meredith wasn't a selfish, insane bitch. She was all right with Becca fucking anyone the roommate wanted. However, in this case, bringing it up constantly to piss Meredith off, sheds light on a pattern that could not be ignored. Meredith assumed the point that the other girl was trying to get across is that Becca was better off than her counterpart because she "made it work" where Meredith chose to end the relationship.

It was common knowledge that Meredith had not believed in monogamy for too long. A strong three or four months was enough to get sick of somebody. And if there was a justification to put an end to the relationship sooner, well, that was even better. It didn't have to be a number. A guy who didn't tip his servers, a chick who couldn't get off her phone for a conversation, or a poor idiot who wasn't ready for a rebound because he wouldn't stop talking about his ex-girlfriend.

Every time she broke it as clean as she could, she went on to the next guy. As long as she was safe and nobody got hurt for a long time, who had the right to comment on what she did? Well, Becca thought she was apparently doing it. She spent the first day after the fall, being so complacent about how bad she looked, how she didn't know how it happened. Anyone would think that being so apologetic meant that she was trying to end the relationship that made her feel so bad.

But that's never the way it went. Every time she was ready to go to visit whatever she was, Becca would ask her over and over if she was okay with Meredith. If it was going through some kind of wall. And every time the answer was the same, no. But Becca could never let the sleeping dog lie. She would almost have been teasing her roommate to tell her that the other one felt some kind of butt hurt. But it never happened. Meredith would not have offered satisfaction to that skank.

That's not the worst part, though. That came when Becca was going to go into detail about whatever Meredith and the ex broke up. She would have made it seem like it was a non-issue, and to break it up clearly meant that there was something wrong with Meredith, not a relationship. What a fucking'bitch. Here's an example of a conversation like this.

"Mer, you know I 'm surprised you couldn't get over what-his-face mommy issues. I think it's sweet that a guy cares enough about his mother to bring her up during sex. I didn't really mind it. It means he's a nurturing guy! I guess someone who doesn't make a connection has a hard time finding common ground with a guy like that. No offence though."

My favorite Meredith was talking about: "You know Hun, I don't get how you can't make what-his-face cum with your mouth. He's such a hair trigger! I guess some people just have a natural head talent. I 'm sure you 're good though. Maybe that's just the technique you've used."

All this blew up with Becca's childish attitude, and her overall unpleasantness made Meredith ready to leave the sinking ship to the nearest point of the land. This whole scheme came only from the plans Meredith had already set in motion. She found someone looking for a roommate, so she and her new guy were going to get all her shit together on the weekend when Becca was mostly out. And Meredith 's roommate was so focused on herself that she hadn't even noticed that most of Meredith 's stuff was boxed up.

As Meredith thought about how sweet her new roommate was, she felt angry. The plan was to leave without a word, and Becca was stuck with the bill of rent. That's how Meredith will stick her actions to the other girl. But that wasn't enough of that! The penalty did not fit the crime. And to be honest, Meredith knew the stupid girl wasn't going to be able to pay the full amount. While Becca was supposed to pay for how she acted, making her homeless feel serious.

This is when the plan came into view. Meredith would leave her share of the rent and, in return, she would not feel compelled to be merciful to Becca. She was just a little nervous, but Meredith loved being a bitch she wanted to be. It was a simple plan to be sure of that. Meredith is going to make Becca feel like sloppy seconds. She used all these exes to make her roommate feel the second best. And returning the favour would be a lot of fun.

It was a bit of a chore trying to convince her new guy, Matt, to agree to help her out. But he saw a game that could turn into a film, so he was a really big fan of sex games. They often played a role and staged scenes together. This one would have been easy to work with. Meredith knew that her roommate would not resist the chance to throw Becca's "take-down" into her face.

"Mer, hun are you alright? I've heard your talk with Matt, and I just wanted to make sure the two of you are ok?"

It would have seemed so innocent to someone who did not know about Becca 's acts. But Meredith understood, and hearing her roommate's question made her even more adamant about what she had decided to do.

"I 'm sorry you had to overhear that. Mattie and I just broke up."

She might also break herself apart as she spoke to add credibility. Becca placed her hand on Meredith 's shoulder and squeezed it gently. The other girl put it at the same time as a viper coiling her body before striking.

"Oh no sweetie! What happened, you guys have been seeing each other for a couple of weeks, right?"

"Wow, the weird thing is that it felt so real. I thought it was going to be different, but I just couldn't take part in his dirty sexual lifestyle. Stuff he wanted me to do! I'm just not that kind of person."

"I'm so sorry, baby. It will be all right. You know what, do you have some things in his place? I'm going to catch the Uber and go get it so you don't have to. And then you're really going to be done with the man. Give me his number here."

Holy shit, she was really going to fall for it! Meredith sniffed and typed the number of Matt. When Becca got it, she sent a quick text and gave a side hug to her roommate.

"I'm going to take care of it, Mer. You are just going to relax here. I've got some weed in my room if you need to mellow. I'm going to email you when I'm on my way back. I'm not coming home so if I'm gone for a while, don't worry about it."

Meredith received a text when the other girl got up and stepped into her bedroom.

The text was opened as soon as the door closed. Matt had given her a screen shot of Becca 's email.

"Becca: Yeah, Matt. This is Becca, the roommate of Meredith. Do you have a second to talk?

Matt was doing it so well. He was meant to look like he didn't want to think about Meredith or get back together.

He didn't want anything to do with his ex, so he was close to doing everything he could to forget about her.

'Matt: Look, if you're here to tell me that breaking up with Meredith was a mistake, you are wasting our breath. I'm not going to give a fuck how she feels. Ok, I 'm done with her.

'Becca: No, this is me texting just to check on YOU. I know how self-righteous and demanding she can be at times. I love her to death but it gets old very quick. Do you need somebody to talk to? I'm swinging by Wendy's and thought maybe I should check in for some nuggets?'

'Matt: I don't really think chicken and tequila nuggets go together. Why don't you come over and bring something to drink?'

Meredith sat back with a smirk at how well this was falling into place. It was almost sad how effortlessly she had duped her roommate into going along with all of this.

'Becca: LOL sure I'll bring you some liquors by. Anything specific?'

'Matt: Yeah, pick up some 1800, just anything but coconut. Yo, why are you doing this?'

'Becca: It's awkward. I know we've only met like 4 or 5 times but I really like you. I just didn't attempt anything cause I love Meredith like a sister. But if she can't see what an awesome guy you are, maybe you'll let me fill that position?'

'Matt: Wow, I had zero idea. We should perhaps talk about it more when you get here. U know exactly where I'm at?'

'Becca: nah, shoot me the address. do we have to talk? I can certainly think of nice things we can do with our mouths'

The evocative wink Becca ended her texted which made her roommate seethe. What a bitch! They hadn't even been broken up for I hour and this was Becca's reaction.

'Matt: oh damn. Are you really suggesting what I think you are?'

'Becca: Well this might not be completely true but the best way I've found to forget someone is to get under someone else. And you can definitely get under me. Btw my Uber would be here soon. '

Again with the evocative emojis. This bitch really had zero shame. Meredith got up and knocked on Becca's bed room door. The smile on her roommate's countenance seemed so indulging.

"Yes, hun?"

"I'm gonna go to my sister's crib for a couple of hours. Need to go out of the house. If I'm not home when you get here just let me know and I'll swing back."

"Ok love. I do hope you feel better. Fuck that guy. Go have real some fun."

If only she understood that. Fuck that guy, huh? You 're betting. Meredith walked out of the house and rushed to Matt's place. He was getting set up there. Meredith saw him handle a pair of handcuffs when she walked in. It was just the sight of them glint that made her pussy clench. She wore it a number of times. Matt had it for that matter. But they'd be around Becca's wrists tonight. The idea was applied to Meredith's quaking.

The lovers had only had enough time for a short shower when Becca said she was outside. Matt told her that the door was open, and she could only come in. Satisfaction bloomed as Becca came in and a surprise came across her face when she saw her roommate. She wasn't doing that, was she?

"Hey Becca! What brings you here?"

She laughed anxiously and hugged the bottle of tequila

in defence.

"Oh, you know! Matt told me that the two of you were beginning to reconcile. I thought that we should celebrate. You know, party and stuff!"

"Oh wow. Really Mattie? You planned this for me, right?"

"Oh, not really baby. Becca came over so we could fuck. Cause me and you weren't together anymore. You remember that?"

"Hey, now that you're saying that I remember trying to break up with you on the phone. Crap, but do you remember why I did that?"

Becca started to shift and tried to speak. Matt cut it off with his response.

"You didn't want to catch your roommate trying to be a traitorous slut. Something like that right?"

Meredith stood up and clapped her hands together loudly.

"You hit Mattie's fucking nail. To catch my roommate trying to screw my ex. Why would you do that, I wonder, Becca? Just to rub in my face that you might succeed with him where I failed? Does getting the one up on me mean so much to you?"

Becca kept moving nervously, and her words came out in stammers.

"Listen to Mer ... honey I was just trying to help you know. I thought Matt could use his shoulder to sob. You guys were broken up anyway. Why does it matter?!"

Meredith walked slowly towards her friend, and with each step the other girl looked more and more like a cornered rabbit.

"It doesn't matter to Becca because you're not fucking my exes because you're horny. Which I might easily excuse, even encourage. You 're doing it because you want to rub it in my face. And that I can't bear. I refuse to let you disrespect me like this anymore. I want to know what your lesson is going to be like?"

Becca tried to speak, but she was quickly silenced by a swift attack by Meredith to her left ear. She let out a little cry, but she remained silent.

"I 'm going to fuck you Becca. And then Mattie here is going to fuck you. Since you love my sloppy seconds, you should be more than excited to join the band. Now, you 're going to come to the bedroom willingly, or I'm going to have to make you."

Becca was silent. She didn't take any steps to Meredith or the bed room, so Matt crossed the room to grab her.

He lifted it over his shoulder cave man's style and put it in his bed space. The other girl followed him with a smile. The tingle between her legs had never let up. When she came to her roommate, she laid back on the bed with her hands.

Matt came behind his lover and began to strip him of her. Becca had been secretly envious of her roommate's body since she first moved in. Meredith had the natural curves and the big round, large breasts that made men drool. That being coupled with her curly long black eyes and startling blue eyes made Becca's roommate quite a small number. It was humiliating to be captured, but the thought of getting fucked by Meredith and her lover was certainly helping with that.

Becca watched Matt's hands move up and down her roommate's body slowly. While doing this they were also stopping at each other's sensitive spots. Seeing her naked roommate and hearing Meredith 's soft groans, she began to add an anticipation to Becca's pussy coating.

"Touch Becca, get yourself ready."

To Meredith 's surprise, Becca obediently spread her bent legs and rubbed the excitement on her pussy lips. They were puffy and purple. The lovers waited, and as Becca kissed, Matt helped Meredith step into her harness ring. She smirked as the eyes of her roommate widened at the sight of it. The 8-inch toy was as big as the soda can be. After Matt put a condom on the toy and rubbed a little rubber on it, he sat on his knees behind Becca. He held her wrists, and while she was fixed on the glowing monster behind her legs, he clapped his handcuffs on her.

Becca looked up at his smirking face and balked at the mischievous look that she saw there. Matt pulled her hands back and was able to slip her bound hands behind his back. Effectively locking her in there.

"Becca, keep your eyes on me. I want to see your slutty face while I fuck you."

The other girl gave a nod of demure and clasped her hands together. Without giving her time to prepare, Meredith sank the tool into Becca 's pussy to the hilt. The rounded end that had slipped into Meredith jumped with the first thrust causing her to groan softly. Becca's uproar, however, drowned it. Meredith pulled back all but the last few inches and slipped the whole length back home with a smirk. Her roommate gasped again, shifting inside the bulk of her.

Meredith 's eyes never left her roommate's as she speeded up her pace. The sound of Becca's wet pussy and the lubricating tool mingled with her moans and her roommates groaning. Meredith placed her thumb over Becca's swollen little clit and rubbed the circles against her delicate little nub. The moans of her roommate rose and her hips moved up to deepen the pressure. Becca 's eager whimpering has driven her roommate to press faster and harder. Each stroke moves the prong inside her, causing her heavy breasts to bounce.

"I think it's time to turn this bitch over, huh Mattie?"

Matt gave a malicious grin and leaned back so that his legs went up and Meredith could pull Becca's cuffed hands from underneath him. After she was home, the other girl turned to her stomach.

"On your hands and knees, there's a cock in front of you that needs attention."

She looked up and her mouth dropped open to the cock she was facing. Matt's seven inches was tough and throbbing to watch his lover fuck another girl. One as different from Meredith as Becca was. She was a tall, blonde, blond, girl-type volleyball surfer. High and slightly muscled. He bent it towards her waiting mouth, and she accepted it willingly. The wet warmth of her mouth made Matt groan and push forward.

Becca was effectively managing the impressive limb in her mouth when she felt a hand on the back of her head. Meredith was about to force her roommate's mouth further down her lover's cock. Just as the other girl started to choke Meredith, she jammed the toy back into the wet cunt in front of her. Her eyes had been on her boyfriend. She shook at the look on his face. Every time Meredith forced her roommate's mouth down Matt, she groaned loudly and bit her lip. It was so sexy to see him like that.

After ten or so minutes, Matt began shaking, and his lover may have ended up coming for him. She moved Becca's head harder, and her lovers' eyes locked as Matt climaxed. Meredith holding the head of her roommate so that none of it would be lost. She pulled her roommate back by her tied hands.

When Becca turned to face the other girl, she never flinched when she felt lips against her own. She grabbed Meredith 's soft hips and leaned to the touch. How many times did Becca think about lip closure with her roommate? Too many to remember that. But as she deepened, she realised that Meredith was not kissing her for the act. She was looking for her mouth. For Matt's cum, Becca could feel her roommate's tongue ringing and blinking for a trace of it.

Matt helped his lover out of the strap harness, and the two of them moved in. Becca found herself on her back again. Meredith was on her left side, and Matt was between her thighs.

"Becca, take a look at me."

The girls met her eyes, and Meredith smiled at her roommate.

"Open your mouth now."

Meredith thought it would be a job to convince Becca to behave during this time, but the other girl was strangely compliant. She opened her mouth and kept it open as Meredith straddled her face.

"You 're such a good Becca girl. Have you always been such a submissive slut? I wonder if you let all my exes fuck you like that."

Matt looked into his lovers' face and smirked as he saw her eyes on his face. She loved to be watched. And she was happy to oblige her lover. He rolled on a condom and kept watching his beautiful lady. As Meredith began to roll her hips, Matt bent his cock down and slipped into Becca 's pussy. The vibrations from her moaning radiated to Meredith, and caused the other girl to bear to get more of that feeling.

Becca tasted the pussy of her roommate and started to lap her tongue up and down. As she moaned, she realized that Meredith had ground her hips tighter, but Becca didn't hold back any noise. But the way Matt was playing, she couldn't hold back even if she wanted to.

And when Becca swirled her tongue around her roommate's pulsating clit, the other girl's thighs shook slightly against her head.

The pace began to accelerate as the combined throttle of noise reached its peak. Meredith was basically humping her roommate's mouth, each push that caused her body to suck as it approached the end. Matt's been in the same position. Each of his thrusts shook the bed frame, and Becca shook along with it. The sound that hit the wall was almost loud enough to cover the cacophony of moans and screams.

"I 'm going to cum baby! Will you clean it up for me?"

Meredith did not have enough time to answer as her body clenched tightly and her legs clamped around her roommate's back. Becca could feel the other girl bouncing and shaking as a rush of liquid coated her mouth and slid down her cheeks. Matt was just behind her. He rushed to get his cock out and take the condom off. His eyes remained on his orgasm lover as he stroked the pelvis of Becca and the hood of her pussy to the full.

Meredith was the first to move around. She fell to the side, still breathing heavily. Matt followed suit and sat down beside Becca's prone body.

"Look at the mess you left with Mattie, and you want

me to clean it up?"

Becca didn't hear Matt's reply. Yet she felt the tongue of her roommate against her pelvis. The warm feeling of being exposed to the rapidly cooling cum pools made Becca curl her legs. And she couldn't contain the gasp in Meredith 's mouth, stroking over her unrelieved clit. She began to think that Meredith would never let go of her cum.

After Becca had showered, the three of them got into Meredith's car and began driving back to the girls' apartment. Nobody spoke during the journey, but what would any of them actually say? Becca was quiet because she was still shocked about what had happened. Moments on a slideshow in her head. Since the first time they met each other more than a year ago, she had been eager for her roommate. It was even more than her visions had indicated.

When they pulled in front of the apartment, Meredith handed the envelope to Becca, who was sitting in the back.

"I 'm moving out. This is next month's check-in rental and some extra money for groceries and shit like that. I 'm going to be around the weekend to pick up my stuff. You 're going to have a month to find a new roommate."

Becca stared at the envelope, and then at Meredith in

the rear-view mirror. A sad, helpless look shone in her eyes. No, Meredith had already made her decision. She wouldn't have gone back to it now.

"Get out of here."

The last time Becca looked at Meredith, she saw the determination in her eyes. She got out of the car and slowly moved to the apartment building. Meredith was driving away without even seeing if the other girl had even gone to the house. Then, she didn't feel anything. Matt broke her attention on the road as he plugged his phone into the car, and his music began to play softly. It was a song that Meredith liked, too.

"Damn, all that shit left me hungry like hell. Let's get some fucking Burger King."

Meredith took a quick look at him and smiled at the cars in front of her. Her boyfriend had just helped her take revenge by screwing her "ex" friend, and now he was dreaming about getting burgers. She would be able to get out of this new one for more than a few months.

The Evening of Erotic

I took the bar exam with Jasmine and Amber. Amber was a mutual friend of ours who had done her internship in her own family's law firm, but we had both known her since college. Luckily, all three of us passed the multistate Bar Exam. So, we decided to celebrate the outcome together. We planned our own special celebration to be held after a ritual family lunch. Our plan was to have an evening of erotic diversion after months of preparation and intense study. Jasmine had convinced us to go to a special erotica club normally reserved for couples; however, unaccompanied girls were always welcome. It was a place that she had discovered by chance with Amelia. Amelia, as Jasmine told it, was always looking for new adventures.

"I just need to make a phone call and we'll have everything we could want," Jasmine told us to convince us to accept.

"But first let's go get a toast to ourselves," Amber suggested.

"Go for a toast and the club." I finished staring at the six o'clock appointment in Amber's apartment.

By pure coincidence, I met Jasmine in front of Amber's door, discovering that not only were we dressed in almost the same way, with solid-color minidresses, I diverted some because unlike her I was not wearing an emerald green; however, our shoes were similar, black patent leather pumps with similar high heels and a clutch.

"I wonder how that bitch, Amber got dressed," Jasmine said to me while we were getting into the elevator obviously a little annoyed at our similar dressing style. I supposed that we should have tried to coordinate our outfits to avoid this.

Amber Simmons, was also known as Red in college, due to the natural color of her hair. She was also called that because she had somewhat of a reputation for being a slut and there was that old Prince Song, "Little Red Corvette" which made us think of her as she was kind of a fast girl. She was the only heir to her family that had been lawyers practically since the profession was founded. The main rumor about Amber was that she passed more exams by opening her legs than opening books. And someone once told me that she had been involved in a BDSM relationship with one of the tenured professors at the university, a professor that was known for being a hardass. As a present for getting into law school, her parents paid for a swanky apartment for her where she often held large parties where sex was pretty much a guarantee. Although all of these were mainly rumors to me as I had rarely attended any of the parties, I was much too busy studying.

As I rang the bell, Amber opened and showed off a bold look. She was wearing a dress that practically showed herself off like a streetwalker. She wore a miniskirt and a transparent blouse that exposed her bra.

"Paige is this the first time you've been to my apartment," Amber asked, giving me a kiss on the cheek that made me think she felt bad for me having never been there before.

"Yes, but I don't think it will be the last," I replied, passing a hand behind her head to kiss her back, sticking my tongue in her mouth.

"Well, hello to you too," Jasmine said sarcastically, feeling a little left out. She closed the door.

In response, I kissed her as well as I had with Amber, but much longer, and then we went to sit at her breakfast nook which had tall bar stools. Amber immediately opened a bottle of champagne, so we started toasting but the atmosphere started to become very sexy. Jasmine and I languidly glanced at each other and Amber kept running her finger over her lips.

With the second bottle began the kisses that became increasingly bold, especially those with Amber, who at one point left her stool to take off her blouse and stand between Jasmine and me.

"Do you want to play a game," she proposed between kisses.

"Why not," I replied, feeling her bottom.

She took two small straps which she attached to our necks, to which she attached a leash with a lobster clasp. Then she put on some dance music and made us stand up, and told us to stand a couple of feet from each other.

"Let's see how good you are at dancing," she said, sitting back on the stool.

It was enough for me to move very little to pick up the minidress and find myself with my thong in plain sight. She did not seem amused enough, so I began to touch myself, passing a finger continuously over my thong, imitated almost immediately by Jasmine, who quickly reduced the dress to a band that covered only her belly. Although I was tied with a collar, I didn't feel at all submissive to the person who was leading the game, but I enjoyed exciting it by moving with all the sensuality I was capable of.

My purple thong soon became almost black as it was soaked, but then even those of the other two girls were certainly not dry. Amber for her part played at pulling and releasing the leashes, until she made us get so close to her, to allow me to touch Amber.

"You don't need this anymore," I told her as I unleashed my leash, before slipping my hands under her miniskirt and uncovering her buttocks.

"Not even this," said Jasmine, taking off her collar after taking off her bra.

"You are really two horny girls," ruled Amber dropping my ground. "Now I have an urge to take your ass, but only if you promise me that after you will do the same with me."

"Now that it's a good program. "I replied, rubbing her butt against my leg. "And then it's so much better that I don't take it properly."

Surely it was the champagne that made all three of us uninhibited, but then there was no room in that room. they were certainly three beauties, but also three women willing to make new experiences. Also, the last one to sodomize me was Hugh, but from that day several ago, after which I had granted myself only to Brett.

Without ever ceasing to touch our lower backs we found ourselves in Amber's room, where she ordered us to crawl onto the bed. As I went on all fours, she lowered my thong to make me feel her tongue on that small strip of skin that separates the two doors of pleasure.

"You really have a nice ass," she said, brushing my little hole. "But Jasmine's is spectacular."

In fact, my friend really had an amazing backside, so much so as to give a new meaning to the term PAWG or phat ass white girl, and Amber soon abandoned mine to devote herself to that of Jasmine. But I didn't want to stay too far apart, so I turned around to be able to sink my tongue between Jasmine's buttocks, who slipped a couple of fingers inside her anus like a real slut as if to invite us to follow her example.

"Take this handle off," Amber told her, slapping her hand, then replacing Jasmine's fingers with hers.

"Look how wet the slut is," I exclaimed a little later as I slipped a couple of fingers into Jasmine's wet hole. "Come on Amber, let us take a couple of fake dicks that we'll fuck her for good."

Amber grabbed my idea, and almost threw on the bed some dildos of different sizes and shapes.

"This seems made for your ass," said Amber to Jasmine while sodomizing her with a dildo made from different spheres of the same size.

We both found ourselves licking my colleague's vagina, while the redhead kept buggering her with a very little femininity.

"Take one and screw her," Amber suggested, pointing to the toys she had taken out of her drawer.

I grabbed a very realistic but above all very big phallus, which I slipped into Jasmine after rubbing it against mine.

"You are bitches and nothing else, so I will cum right away," Jasmine shouted, prey to unbridled pleasure.

Amber and I didn't listen to her at all, on the contrary, she almost started a competition for those who fucked her with more force, while we touched each other without any restraint. In those moments I wanted nothing more than to take Jasmine's place and experience the same enjoyment, and when I saw her reach orgasm, I did not slow down even for a second, in fact, I increased the rhythm a little making her scream with pleasure.

"Damn, you're a fury," exclaimed Amber, perhaps amazed by my aggression. "But now why don't you dedicate yourself to me too?"

I pushed the redhead on the bed and then kissed her

with all the passion I had, trying at the same time a little of anger because I wanted to be in her place, so I took the phallus and penetrated her completely with a single lunge, suffocating her moans with my mouth.

"Jasmine put something in her ass, but make sure it is big or this bitch won't even feel it."

"Would you say this one is enough or do I have to look for a bigger one," Jasmine answered me, brandishing a big phallus with a handle.

"I don't know, in the meantime, throw it inside, then let's see how much she enjoys it."

Amber, not at all frightened by our sentences, tried to bring her feet as close as possible to her head, so as to favor double penetration, but Jasmine wanted to delay. In fact, while I continued to screw her, without forcing the pace too much, Jasmine began to lick her little hole and then slip a finger in it, and immediately started using the tongue again.

"Just please." Amber whispered, "so it's too exciting."

"Tell me you want me to screw your ass and do it well," Jasmine replied, teasing her anus with a finger.

"Come on let me enjoy."

"No no, not so." Jasmine said placing a hand on mine

to slow me down "You have to say it WELL!"

"Please put it in my ass and let me enjoy it like a slut, break it in two as you see fit do what you want to me."

"That's better, "the blonde replied. "Now let's see how slutty you really are."

Jasmine placed the tip of the phallus against Amber's anus, then slowly brought in only the tip, but when it was inside, she pushed the bat with all her strength, making the woman scream with pain. But Amber didn't tell her to stop or even slow down, but she waited for all that pain to turn into pleasure until she groaned at our every lunge.

"Man, how slutty you are," Jasmine told her suddenly "It's okay that at the university you gave it to everyone, including Professor Khan who is a real pig who takes the girls home, to have them with that big bitch of his wife. Maybe you also made it with Professor Logiti, but don't fuck anybody because he can't take it anymore, but on the other hand, he likes to watch while some handsome black guy fucks his students who are eager to take thirty."

" Yes, only Prof. Logiti he screwed two men that didn't have normal cocks but two monstrous clubs. He pretty much came as soon as he touched it, but those two really broke me in two. For Professor Khan, I had to lick his wife's snatch for as long as he was fucking me, not knowing that the pig was Viagra stoned," she told Jasmine.

I was shocked to know how many professors, all of them respected, had exchanged grades for 'sexual favors'. That so many of them had involved the students also in relationships with each other, while I had had to work hard to get my good grades. They were also talking about two teachers known for their seriousness and severity, but who evidently hid who knows how many perversions behind the facade. At the same time, however, I was almost envious of the two girls' adventures, not knowing whether or not to regret having been a model student.

Eventually even Amber had her orgasm, which was much more violent than Jasmine's, and almost with some embarrassment, I found myself on my knees between my two friends, who were just waiting for me to give myself to them.

"I passed all the exams without giving it to anyone," I said almost looking for the reason why I was different from them.

"I know, but now you put yourself on all fours and be quiet so that we will screw you properly even if you were a saint at the university," Amber answered giving me a kiss.

So, I got on all fours, and immediately their tongues took possession of both my mount of wetness and my ass, making me very excited in a short time. I started to moan louder and louder, but without having the courage to ask for anything more, not knowing what they would do to me. It was Amber who took a vibrator and passed it several times along the gap in my vagina until I begged her to screw me. But it was not she who penetrated me, but Jasmine who sodomized me with a long, thin dildo, before Amber put the vibrator into me.

"Go until I cum," I screamed as if to get relieve myself of the burdens of being a prude in college. "From today I just want to enjoy without thinking of anything else."

"I knew that behind that face a virgin was hiding a slut in full form," Amber answered giving me a small slap on the butt "And don't worry with me and this blonde bitch you will enjoy everything just fine."

"Whore of the week," exclaimed Jasmine before dropping a little of saliva above my little hole. "In two years at the law firm, I saw her having sex with men and women without any problems. Paige is one who may have woken up late, but is recovering quickly."

The two continued to screw me, slowing down every time I approached orgasm, but when I finally came it was like a real explosion of pleasure, which I was left exhausted on the bed for several minutes, without strength, only able to breathe.

"Why do not you tell me before about Prof. Khan and his wife," Asked Jasmine to Amber sitting on the bed. "Later, you can tell me what you did with his wife. Did you ever happen to go to the gym that recruits handsome boys to take to bed, sometimes, I left with two."

Red replied, "If we start talking, we will skip the entire evening out, even if I saw that we can do without the men and enjoy the same."

I burst out laughing, immediately followed by the other two colleagues, only to find ourselves talking about our experiences without any taboos, stopping only for a quick pizza and ending up have so much good sex when we found ourselves too excited.

First Time Anal Sex with the Boss

When curvy redheaded Wendy thinks about Coleman, her boss, she can't help but think that she is just not his type. When she puts together a terrific event for him and his clients, he repays her in ways she never saw coming.

I was cursed with a sexy boss. I know, that does not really seem like a curse, but it was. He was a constant distraction with his wavy black hair and deep brown eyes. And sometimes he would even take off that suit jacket, loosen the tie and unbutton that top button at his throat, and roll up those shirt sleeves. His forearms were nicely toned and muscled without being bulky or veiny. You could just tell that his whole body was probably just as flawless.

All the women in the office swooned over him, and he was definitely the topic of conversation over the coffee pot almost every morning. They wanted all the dirt from me, but I was steadfast in my loyalty. Being his assistant had certain perks, but since I really needed the job, I could not afford to spread his secrets around the office.

There was not anything really dirty. Maybe a little naughty, but nothing you would not expect from a gorgeous thirty-year-old successful investment banker. He would sometimes ask me to send flowers or gifts to his dates slash one-nighters, but that really was not all that strange. I did sometimes look up the women he sent them too, and they all pretty much looked the same. They were all on the tall side and of course slender with long blonde hair and blue eyes that always held the same vacant look. It was too cliché for words actually. Even with all of my access, I knew there was no place in his world for a short, curvy redhead with green eyes. I was pretty much the opposite of his type.

That sure did not stop me from fantasizing about him. In my dreams at night, we were the hottest item at the company, and everyone was envious of the way he looked at me. And of course, lots and lots of red hot steamy sex. In the office, in the car, in the five-star hotel downtown, on a private island. But I digress…

Seeing as I have been single for the last nine months with nary a date in sight, my loneliness (and horniness) may have contributed to the dreams. My friends did not believe me when I told them just how hot he was, so one day I 'borrowed' his professional head shot from the computer files and texted it to a couple of them. They both swooned until my phone smoked from the lewd comments.

Luckily for me, I am a very good assistant to him. And

while he seems to be a little bit arrogant, I guess he has the right to be – gorgeous and successful men usually do. But he treated me well enough, and would sometimes send me home early or give me gift cards for lunches out. He never took me to lunch, but I guess I would ruin his image or something. I mean, he was the kind of man that looked cool eating a cocktail shrimp in his charcoal gray suit while I was the kind of woman that ended up with cocktail sauce down the front of my white cardigan.

Whenever we have office functions, he made a point to chat with me before circulating with the 'important' folks. I appreciated the attention, and not just because the other assistants would flock over to whisper and giggle over him. I tried to maintain my professional demeanor, but if the function included alcohol, I sometimes got giggly too.

One day he pulled me into his office to discuss a project. I grabbed my notepad and pen and headed in to see him. I felt the butterflies flutter inside my tummy when he grinned at me. He was leaned back in his chair, suit jacket off, tie off, sleeves rolled up. His dark hair looked slightly ruffled, as though he had been running his fingers through it and his brown eyes threw copper sparks in my direction. He was definitely up to something.

"Hi Coleman," I gave him a friendly but professional smile.

"Hey there Wendy," he gestured to one of the chairs that waited in front of his desk.

"I'm hoping you can help me with a client function."

"Sure, what did you have in mind?" It was not that unusual of a request.

"Well, I was thinking of something off-site, hopefully with a private space and a bar and catering."

"For how many people?" I jotted notes down quickly.

"Maybe twenty or so? A few colleagues from here and some of our top clients. We need this to be top shelf."

"Sure, I can look into some options and get back to you."

"Perfect. Oh, and I'd like you to attend as well. If these are our top clients, they need to know you as well. Sometimes I can be hard to get in touch with, so they need to know my assistant."

I flushed pink, "O-Ok, I understand."

I sat back down at my own desk and sighed. Although the firm pays well, 'top shelf' was not a lifestyle I could keep up with. And it sounded like he wanted me to go all out, within reason. I had my work cut out for me it seemed. I started looking into a few of the fancy bars that I was aware of, but none of them seemed right. I wanted to make an impression with this project, and I needed something unique. I started trolling the nightlife websites and restaurant reviews, and came up with a few options that seemed to be in line with what he was looking for. I even saved their catering menus to review, and fired off several emails to the respective event managers at the venues.

It was the end of the day, so I packed it up. Unfortunately, all of those menus had made me hungry so I made plans and met up with a friend at a nearby Mexican place for tacos and queso. She was 'in the know' on the fancy life because of her highly connected concierge job, so I picked her brain over margaritas.

****

My friend and I came up with a short list of venues for me to check out, so I actually spent the next day away from the office visiting all of them. None of them were my style, so I was not really sure even how to dress. I chose a simple gray suit just to be on the safe side.

The first place was a regular looking bar inside a hotel. The prices were outrageous, for the space and the food and the drinks, and there did not appear to be anything special about it. The second place was a little better, cost wise, but still rather plain to look at. It certainly did not 'wow' me, and I was not a client who planned to give the investment firm hundreds of thousands of dollars. They were at least nice enough to provide me with a free lunch, though. I promised to keep them in mind for future functions.

The third place knocked it out of the park, though. It was also in a downtown hotel, but the bar itself had a private express elevator right off the lobby, and the facility took up the entire roof. It had a panoramic view of the entire skyline, several bars to gets drinks, cocktail tables, and a dance floor. I could see that the wooden gables were all strung with tiny white lights which probably looked amazing at night. The catering manager for the hotel arrived to talk with me as I was touring the place. We reviewed the menu, and she seemed to be more than happy to work with us so that we stayed on budget. I was thrilled with the choice, and took all my information back to the office to discuss it with Mr. Sexy Boss.

I arrived at the office around three in the afternoon, and gathered my notes so that I could pretend to sound intelligent to the boss. He seemed pretty happy with my choice and we decided on a menu for the event after deciding on a date. He also gave me a list of people to email and invite personally. Luckily, I was able to create a form letter and just replace the name.

We had scheduled the event for a Saturday night which was perfect because I had plenty of time to get ready. I really wanted to knock the boss's socks off, professionally and personally.

I grabbed takeout on my way home that Friday night, and went to sleep early. No one looks good with heavy bags under their eyes. That Saturday morning, I slept in and took a leisurely time getting ready. I did finally leave the house to pick up my dress from the dry cleaners, and get my toenails painted. I hate having my fingernails painted, so I just left them plain. When I got home, I even took a small nap after my turkey sandwich. When I got up, I took a nice long shower, scrubbing and shaving everything from the neck down. A little scented lotion and I got to work on my crazy hair.

About thirty minutes later, I had the whole mess tamed into a French twist with loose waves escaping against my cheeks. I do not normally wear makeup, so even applying a bare minimum, I looked all fancy in the mirror. I slipped into my emerald cocktail dress, and chose a pair of dangly silver earrings and strappy silver sandals to finish the outfit. With my silver purse in hand, I headed to the event a little early to make sure everything was good to go.

Coleman was already there when I arrived, and by the wide-eyed stare, I must have looked pretty good. I greeted him and then clicked around on my high heels to check everything. The twinkly little lights made the whole space look like a fairy garden, and the tables were set with crisp white linens. The food smelled amazing, and my tummy rumbled as I passed the tray of warm crab cakes.

"I'm not sure, but I think we need to test the food and the bar before anyone else gets here," Coleman's deep voice rumbled behind me.

I jumped in surprise, and whirled around on my heels. This little maneuver may look great on other people, but for me, it just set me off-balance, and I ended up having to brace myself against his very solid chest. The copper dress shirt set off his chocolate eyes perfectly, and I found myself lingering a little too long.

He grinned down at me, and I pulled away sharply.

"I'm so sorry," I mumbled.

"Quite alright. How about a drink while we wait?"

When we turned together to walk to the nearest bar, I felt his warm hand on my lower back, escorting me in front of him. My whole body shivered at his touch, and I just tried to play it cool. Not one of my strong points, but I like to pretend.

"What would you like?" he gestured to the bartender.

"Vodka cranberry, extra limes," I rattled off my order with practiced ease.

"Ah, straight to the hard stuff," he chuckled, "I can support that. Two fingers of Scotch, neat. And thanks, my good man."

Eventually, the guests started arriving, and Coleman moved off to mingle. I tried to stay out of the way as best I could, and just watched him in action. I did manage to help myself to the crab cakes as well as the marinated mushrooms, the cheese display, and the cocktail shrimp. Unfortunately, I also continued to help myself to the bar.

By the time everyone started trickling out, I think I had had at least four or so. I snagged one last crab cake, and made my way over to Coleman.

"Excellent shindig," he grinned at me, "you did a great job."

"Oh, thank you, sir." I hoped I didn't slur.

"Can you hold on a moment while I finish settling up?"

"Certainly."

After he signed the final tab and whispered something to the staff member, he walked back over to me with a strange and intense look on his face. I was not sure why, but suddenly I felt like prey.

****

Coleman was stalking towards me intently, and my instinct was to back away. But when I looked at him, with his dark wavy hair and strong jawline, I realized that I would be insane not to find out what he was thinking. I gripped my tumbler tightly as he grew closer.

He stopped just a foot in front of me, and firmly removed the glass from my hand. I surrendered it to him mostly out of confusion. He set the glass down on the nearby table and looked back at me.

"Wendy?" he asked quietly, letting his warm hand slide over my trembling fingers.

"Yes? Coleman?" I was so confused.

His hand was still sliding up my arm and over my shoulder until it stopped at the nape of my neck. With his lips just inches from mine, I caught the warm scent of Scotch.

"You look stunning tonight," he whispered.

I was still awestruck that he was speaking to me, but

he took my breath away when I felt his lips meet mine. I inhaled sharply as his other hand curved around my waist. At first, my arms were frozen to my sides, but as the tip of his tongue tickled my upper lip, I threaded my arms around his neck.

The silent acceptance of his advance spurred him into action. His teeth closed lightly on my bottom lip, and he pulled me fully against his body. He was as firmly muscled as I had imagined, and even if I wanted to escape, I probably could not have done so successfully.

The hand on my neck slowly threaded into my curly up-twist, while the hand at my waist slid downward to cup my ass. I was silently grateful that (a) I had shaved and (b) I had worn some of my sexy panties. His tongue sought entrance to my mouth, and I parted my lips to him.

As our tongues danced together, he pushed me backwards until I was up against the table. The edge dug into my rounded ass until he lifted me up onto the table and nestled between my legs. The full skirt of my cocktail dress flowed around both of us until we were pressed against each other again. I could feel a distinct pressure against me, but I was not sure if that was him or just me being optimistic.

His hair was thick and soft between my fingers as I ran one hand up the back of his head. When his lips slid along my jawline and down my throat, I took a hurried glance around the open space. There was no one around, even the wait staff had disappeared. All I could see was the twinkling white lights and the illuminated skyline just beyond the edge of the space. It was a surreal night in a fairy tale setting.

Coleman raked his nails up the outsides of my thighs, dragging the skirt with his hands. My thighs tingled with anticipation in the cool night air, and I gasped at the breeze that tickled my skin.

"God, you're unbelievable," he mumbled as his tongue traced my collarbone, "why has have I resisted this long…"

"Wait, what?"

He chuckled, "You have no idea how long I've wanted to do this, to touch you, to feel you."

"Coleman! Really?"

He slowly slid the straps of my dress off my shoulders, letting the dress drape loosely around my tits. The rounded swell of my cleavage rose and fell with each breath I took, and he was almost mesmerized. His large hands cupped the outer curves, pressing them up and together until the dress could no longer hold them. The dress slipped free, and my tits spilled out into his hands. He looked up at me with a gleeful look in his dark eyes, and then buried his face in the warm valley of my flesh.

I was still awestruck that he had ever considered me in that way. I had seen pictures of his dates before, the skinny blondes with no curves whatsoever. But he seemed so excited to be caressing my soft roundness.

He caught my rosebud nipples between his fingers and tugged them gently, tightening them into stuff aching peaks. Back and forth his tongue flicked from one to the other, teasing and tormenting them from his warm mouth to the cool evening breeze. By the time he cupped them with his palms, I was shivering and gasping.

My boss raised his head to look me square in the face, his own gaze darkened with desire. While still staring into my eyes, his hands slowly crept under my dress until they were tickling along the hems of my panties. I was squirming and desperate to break the intense stare, but he refused to let me. When I would start to turn away, he would withdraw his hands. When I would look back at him, the teasing resumed.

He traced one fingertip along the damp spot at the

center of my silk panties and grinned at me. He pressed a little harder with the next pass, dragging a moan from my lips. I was squirming and wriggling on the table in front of this gorgeous dark-haired boss while he teased my aching pussy.

I still was not sure what exactly was going to happen next. At least, I was not sure until he took my hand and pressed it to the front of his slacks. I squeezed lightly and discovered that my previous optimism was no fantasy; it was reality. Even through his clothing, I could feel that he was thick and long and ready for me. I slid my cupped hand up and down the shaft, and he thrust his hips into my touch.

With a boldness that I did not know I possessed, I slowly popped open the button and drew the zipper down. He exhaled sharply as the tiny vibrations radiated into him, and his cock bobbed free as soon as the zipper reached the bottom.

"Coleman," I whispered throatily, "do you mean to tell me you've been commando all night?"

He grinned wickedly, "I'm always commando. You just never know…"

He was hard and ready, with full balls still nestled in his slacks. I tickled the head of his cock with my fingernails, making it bob and jerk. I slowly ran my fingertips up and down the shaft lightly, watching his face as I teased him. His hips pushed towards my hand, but I pulled back, keeping my touch faint and just firm enough for him to feel.

"Oh God," he moaned, his eyes rolling back in his head.

With a wicked grin of my own, I slid off the table, my tits bouncing with my movements. I knelt gently on the floor with his cock right in front of my face. It was as magnificent as I had fantasized about. Long and thick and hard, throbbing just for me.

I ran my tongue up the underside of the shaft and closed my lips around the head. As it pulsed hotly against my tongue, I tasted his need. I ran my tongue in slow swirls over the head, finding each sensitive spot that made his abs tighten in anticipation. Just as I thought he was going to come unglued, I slid my mouth down further, letting it meet my fingers that encircled the base.

He was completely enclosed in warmth. My fingers spread the dampness around as I slid up and down his cock, enveloping him in the wetness from my mouth. Coleman leaned forward and braced himself on the table as I continued to suck his cock. I worked my free hand inside his open trousers and cupped his balls.

"Oh yeah, like that," he mumbled, his voice hoarse with

need.

I rolled them with my fingers, squeezing lightly and tickling with my nails.

"Oh fuck," he groaned deeply.

I sped up my stroking while tugging downward on his heavy balls. I felt that telltale final swell in the head of his cock, but my firm grasp on his balls kept his climax from completing.

"Fuck... Wendy..." Coleman moaned again.

I flicked the tip of my tongue against the head of his cock, right at that sensitive spot under the opening, while still stroking with my hand and kneading his balls. He had to have been going crazy. I got my confirmation when I felt his warm hand tangle into my twisted curls. He was pressing downward, not roughly but insistently. With my lips still around the head of his cock, I smiled and obliged.

I released my hold on his full sac, and wrapped both hands around his shaft. With my mouth latched to the head, I stroked him fast and firm while tongue-lashing and sucking the head. His cock pulsed and throbbed several times and then he exploded. My whole body shivered as my gorgeous boss came in my mouth, and my panties were soaked through.

"Oh fuck, fuck, fuck," he groaned loudly.

He finally released the last jet, and withdrew from my mouth. I stood up with to look at him a self-satisfied grin.

"Well, fuck me. If I had known, I would not have waited," he chuckled as he lifted me back to the table.

Coleman worked his hips between my thighs until they were spread open around him. He drove his hands up inside my skirt, and practically yanked my soaked panties from my body. In one smooth motion, he shoved my skirt up nearly to my waist and fell to his knees in front of me.

"You're so wet," he whispered as he stroked my inner thighs.

My whole body trembled with anticipation and need. And I have to admit that I nearly slid off the table when I felt his hot tongue touch my wet flesh. I was immensely grateful that he did not tease me the way I teased him. His tongue dove into me then spiraled up to my aching clit. He drew fast, hard circles and I found my body reacting to him in ways I don't think I had ever felt. I gasped and writhed, clawing at his shoulders. It seemed like only moments before I was crying out to the stars and twinkling lights over my head.

"Coleman!" I screamed as my orgasm quaked through me.

He eased me down slowly and then stood up between my shaking legs.

"Come here," he tugged me gently off the table and spun me around.

He shoved my dress to my waist and caressed my bare ass. I felt his fingers dip between my legs and draw the moisture upwards to my puckered little asshole.

"Coleman? I don't know…"

"Never? I'll be gentle, I promise. I want to feel how tight yours is with my thick cock inside your body."

I whimpered, but his teasing finger did feel nice. He slipped it in slightly, still moving slowly. He eased in and out slowly, eventually adding a second finger. It was a new sensation, but once I relaxed and trusted him, it started to feel nice.

As he continued to play with my ass, he slowly rubbed his shaft along my wet pussy. Once he was good and slick, he pressed the head against me.

"Just relax," he whispered in my ear.

As he pressed forward, I felt his fingers rubbing against my clit. It was just enough of a delicious distraction that

I barely yelped when the head of his cock popped inside me. He slid a thick finger inside my pussy as his cock progressed forward. By the time he was balls-deep in my ass, I was very near my second orgasm. He pumped in and out slowly while continuing to tease my clit. He had me right on the edge but slowed down intentionally.

"I want you to cum with me," I could hear the devilish grin in his tone of voice.

He teased me lightly, keeping me panting on the edge, while his thrusts became quicker and harder.

"Oh you are so tight," he moaned, thrusting firmly inside me.

I could feel his balls slapping against my pussy with each thrust. I reached underneath me and tickled them lightly with my nails.

"Oh shit," he groaned deep in his chest.

I kept tickling, and he kept rubbing my clit.

"Coleman," I moaned.

"I know, me too," he rumbled.

I braced myself on the table with both hands as he thrust fast and erratic into my ass. His fingers still rubbed my clit in time with his thrusts, and I felt my body give in to the pleasure he gave me. I shook and trembled as my climax overtook my senses, and moments later I felt him thrust one last time and then fill me with his juices.

Afterwards, we eventually untangled ourselves and re-dressed. He did snatch my panties away from me and tuck them into his pocket.

"Pervert," I mouthed off as I wrestled my dress back into place.

"You watch that mouth of yours," he grinned.

"You watch it, you've felt what it can do."

Coleman yanked me back to him, flipped my dress up, and swatted my ass hard.

I just looked up at him with a grin, "Harder."

"Oh damn," he rolled his eyes as he zipped his fly.

****

So after all of my self-consciousness around him, it turns out that we were molded for each other. I ended up leaving the firm so that we could date without issues, but he gave me a glowing recommendation for my next position.

We are still together, and when he escorts me to

company functions, it is pretty fun to see all of those other assistants just stare at us when he slides his hands over my ass. Since he goes commando all the time, he prefers it if I am commando around him.

You know, I never much saw myself as the anal type, but with Coleman at the reins, I have learned to love it and all sorts of other new things. Apparently, that swat he gave me that first night was just the tip of the iceberg. Being commando around each other has led to some very steamy trysts in some very random places.

For example, I know that if I stand in a certain way in front of him with one arm back behind myself, I can easily play with his cock in public. Oh, I don't pull it out or anything, but teasing him through his slacks gets him very wound up. I usually get a spanking for being "impertinent" but he just likes to warm my ass up for his cock. And I get an extra swat if I refer to him as 'boss'.

My Show

I saw nothing through the hood over my head but heard all the better. A man's voice sounded somewhat muffled — in the background, the sound of a group of people — muted cheering, tense laughter, expectant murmuring. The male voice gave a story that I could not understand. Only fragments came through intelligibly. However, he worked towards a kind of climax because he started to talk harder and now I could fully understand him: "and here she is... tonight's main show... give her warm applause." "Main show??" That was apparently my key because I was immediately grabbed by several hands and led forward. With my hands tied behind my back and blindfolded eyes, it was a good thing that I was held tight because I stumbled when I was pushed forward. I came to a halt against a sort of cloth. The sound had since swelled into a huge shout and shouts and, indeed, applause. Apparently, I was standing on a stage because the canvas was pushed aside and the cheering became so loud. The whistling and shouting completely drowned out the 'speaking master.' I was pushed forward a few more steps and then slowly turned around a few times. The cheers just got louder. After a while, the speaking master resumed the word, "Here she is tonight's main show. What do you think?"

More shouting and yelling. It was only now that I realized that 'she' was me and that something was going to happen to me on this stage. "Is she good enough...?" even more shouting.

"Is she tasty enough...?" Cries like 'pants off, pants off' now came from the room. The speaker started to praise my body. 'Look what a figure men. Look at those tits...'

The room agreed with him and I felt my breasts feel through my blouse and bra and pinched. Where did I end up? I was turned around and my buttocks got an unqualified speech. My legs were pushed apart and the speaker rubbed my back and my crotch between my legs.

"Is this a nice ass or what?" He closed with firm pets on my buttocks. I felt like a sort of auction piece. The speaking master went on... "Can you see it well enough? is she exposed enough...?" Loud boo now and my stomach turned into a rock. Then we will do something about it! The hands pushed me aside. Something happened because the shouting went crescendo again. Then I felt cold metal glide down my neck, followed by clipping sounds. My blouse was cut open slowly with a large pair of scissors. The room screamed and cheered. After a few cuts, the front was loose. The buildings were kept aside and the speaking master asked the audience what they thought of it. I could go through the ground. To make matters worse, he also squeezed my breasts and asked the room semi-innocently, "And now...?" Loud shouts: "Tits... Tits..."

Immediately my bra at the front was cut. The 'holding hands' also did not allow grass to grow over and pulled him away from me by force. The tape behind my back was cut with the help of a second pair of scissors and in the meantime, the speaking master cut long cuts in the buildings and sleeves of my blouse. In no time, I stood there, naked and perky, piercing my breasts in the shreds of my blouse, blindfolded and bound, on a stage in front of an outrageous crowd. My thoughts strayed to how I ended up here.

It had started a few months ago. Matt, my friend, once asked me about my wildest fantasies. I actually didn't know and wasn't in the mood to think about it, but the question remained. I really started to think about it and gradually I concluded that I am an exhibitionist type. Matt saw that it did not let me go and did not fail to pick my mind regularly. One evening I let go of what I had come up with and it seemed very horny to do something 'public.' I myself had no idea what I meant by it, but it sounded exciting and I noticed that I also found it very exciting to put on my skirt in the car. Passing trucks could then see my slip and that excited me a lot. Matt kept asking what I meant, but I couldn't give him more clarity. A few weeks later, he again attacked me with the following question: "If I organize something for you, will you do it?" "What," I asked, of course. "Well, something public." "Yes Yes, but what then?" I insisted. "Listen," he said, "You either do it, or you don't." The 'what' remains a surprise, just like the when, by the way. You don't have to answer now either, but let us know when you're out.

Furthermore, I cannot say anything, but I promise you that you will not have to do anything against your will and that, as far as I know, you will find it particularly nice, okay? I thought that was reasonable enough and I agreed. Matt said ok and we let it go. In the weeks that followed, it continued to gnaw at me. I was very curious, but every attempt by Matt to provoke a statement did not work out: "Like it or not" was usually the only response. A few weeks later, I told him that I agreed that I could stop or withdraw at any time. That was possible. I got the code word 'redstop.'

If I pronounced that, everything would be immediately interrupted. I had to do it with those words. Furthermore, everything would remain a big mystery. Weeks passed. Nothing happened. I started forgetting the whole incident again. Until one day, I got out of work.

As I walked to my car, I heard footsteps coming after

me. In itself not strange in a large parking garage, but it was late, dark and the footsteps were approaching faster than was reasonable. I turned around and at the same time, the sound stopped. My heart was pounding in my throat and I tried to reassure myself. "Don't put up with it, just someone who has arrived at his car," it didn't help much. In the meantime, I had arrived at my car. I already had my keys in my hand and opened the lock. The moment I open the door, I hear coughing. When I look up, I see a man standing next to me. He smiles kindly and tells me that I can take him to his car (!).

"I didn't think so," I say and with a beating heart, I get into my car. "We thought so," I hear behind me and immediately a second man grabs me and pulls me out of the car. The first conjures up a bag from somewhere and pulls it over my head. I struggle vigorously and try to scream. However, the bag muffles all noise and despite my struggle, the second man clicks on me a few handcuffs. Within a minute, I am bound and blindfolded in another car. The car is going to drive and I am terrified. Sweating heavily in the bag, I start to worry about suffocation. Fortunately, the bag is removed fairly quickly.

The first man sits next to me in the back seat. He still looks at me kindly. "Listen," he says. "Do you remember having a conversation with your friend about fantasies and such?" Something began to dawn on me. "This is the big moment," he continues. We represent a company that realizes all kinds of wishes and desires. You should have agreed on a code word with your friend. Is that right? He gave me ample opportunity to let things sink. I was still thinking about his opening announcements and only after a while did his question come to my mind. "Yes," I said. "Do you remember what it was?" After a long thought, something came to my mind again, "Redstop...?" I asked doubtfully.

"That's right. Good. If you pronounce that word, at any time, it will come to an end and we will bring you back home. Your car is already on its way there, by the way and your friend is aware of everything. If you want, you can call him now." With a questioning look, he handed me a cell phone. I rattled my handcuffs a bit and looked back reproachfully. "Sorry," he said, "Do you promise you're not going to do crazy things?" I nodded and my hands were released and I could call. Matt immediately answered, "How are you, honey?" "Will you continue? Did they not hurt you?" He fired numerous questions, but I did too. After fifteen minutes, everything was clear to everyone and we hung up.

At the same time, I decided to see what was in store for me. A black hood was pulled over my head, but my nose and mouth were released. My hands were handcuffed behind me again and I waited. After an hour's drive, I had to get out and I was led through all kinds of spaces and stairs to finally end up behind a kind of curtain with a loud shout... With a shock, I returned to reality. The cheers dawned on me again and I heard the crowd scream for my pants. I thanked the hood over my head for anonymity and protection. The speaking master further chased the audience and asked my guards to show me. I was lifted up and carried closer to the public. I almost felt the sound. I was turned around and again. My breasts were shown. I imagined splashing against it. The guards squeeze my breasts and shake them back and forth. The crazy audience (it had to be hundreds) screamed for more. And they got that. My guards pulled me back a little and turned my back to the audience. The speaker gave a sign and immediately I was bent over. My counterparts were just futility. I had nothing to say against four strong hands.

They pushed me forward and the speaker came closer talking. Soon I felt his hand stroking my buttocks again. "What do you think about this? Does it sound like something to you?" Shouting and shouting: 'Pants out, Pants out, Pants out.' 'What do you say?' "BROKEN OUT, BROKEN OUT!"

I heard some rolling up the stage. I was lifted up and placed on a platform. My hands were released. I immediately tried to pull away but in vain. Each keeper raised one of my hands and clicked it into a buoy. I was in a kind of frame with my hands high in the air. My ankles were attached to a kind of horizontal beam. I couldn't kick anymore, just standing still. Apparently, the frame was on wheels because I felt how I was being turned around and shown like at a cattle market. The audience still roared about my pants. The speaker approached, cutting his scissors in the air. Although I was wearing sturdy jeans, the scissors had no trouble with it. Just like my blouse, the pipes, and front and back, were cut into long strips from bottom to top. Only my belt held the loose pieces up. Because of the fragments I knew, my slip was now clearly visible. Of course, I just had a thong on that day. Again I was shown and driven back and forth.

The guards kept the cart stopping abruptly so that my shreds of clothing rocked aside. The audience went crazy. The answer was not surprising. Again the scissors came and now my slip was completely cut away. The guards meanwhile removed my shoes and stockings. I was now almost naked on stage with my back to the audience that had a clear view of my ass between the strips of denim. I felt the wind on my body. A fan or something similar fluttered the strips of fabric from my pants and blouse so that the public now had a rich view of me. Then I have slowly turned around and driven back and forth to every corner of the stage. I was shown in detail and the audience screamed even louder for more. In the meantime, the speaker continued to praise me.

'Look at those tits men, ever seen such a beautiful one? Watch those buttocks! Small pets on my buttocks shook my tight ass.

"And what did you think of that pussy? Nice shaved, right?" I felt a hand glide past my landing runway. Involuntarily I withdrew my belly and ass backwards. The code word flashed through my mind. "Then say it, and then say it!" I thought, but another piece thought: "waits a little longer, look at it for a moment..." The audience completely drowned out the speaker. He had apparently pulled his scissors back because I felt the remnant of the shirt sliding off me, followed a moment later by the shreds that once formed my pants. I was completely naked now. Only my belt was still around my waist.

Next to me, I heard some sounds again, followed by something cold that slid down my shoulder. It was slightly liquid and it smelled of... oil! Along with this realization, I heard the speaker ask for four volunteers. Well, there were a hundred of them, but in the end, I heard how some of them climbed onto the stage and ran towards me the fastest. Immediately I felt eight hands smear the oil over me. I was greased from head to toe with the encouragement of their friends in the hall. My initial timidity slowly changed to something... undefined. I noticed that I was not even very shocked when the hands also richly put my buttocks and cat in the oil. One bottle after the other was touched. From my toes to my neck, I was put in a thick layer of oil with particular attention to my breasts and crotch area. I became so slippery that the fingers glided smoothly along and between my labia. Also, between my buttocks went very smoothly and I regularly felt a dot and even rub in my anus.

"Ok, gentlemen," the speaker said. "Thank you for your willing cooperation! It's a dirty job, but somebody has got to do it." The speaker got the laughs on his hand. I felt another hard tap on my buttocks that shook my ass and that were it. Smooth and shiny like an eel; I was once again pulled over the entire stage and shown. I still felt the oil dripping off everywhere. The audience slowly stopped. I suspected that the end had now been reached. What else could happen after all?

I heard some rumbling toward me again. Something on wheels again? The guards detached me from the frame. "Happy," I thought. I survived and was quite proud of myself. They helped me off the stage but did not let me go. I stood with my face to the audience and was pushed with something against my stomach, a sort of high couch, or something. My right ankle was again locked in a buoy. Then they started lashing on my left ankle, pulling my legs apart. I had little choice. When my ankles were completely apart, the left one was also secured. Then I felt how large hands pushed my shoulders forward over the couch. It turned out to be a kind of goat because my breasts fell over it and dangled freely in the air. Then my wrists were pulled down and also secured. I now stood deep down with my legs wide. I just knew that my ass was open and exposed and I felt that my pussy was slightly open. The public had reached the old volume again during this operation. They also suspected what the view would be if I were turned around. The speaker hit the whole thing again on "Turn around?" he asked. "Turn around?" The screams became deafening and I felt how I was slowly being pushed forward. You can hear it all the way to the very edge of the stage. Then, very slowly, centimeter by centimeter, my ass was turned to the audience.

Again the decibel meters were pushed to new values. The speaker fired on the audience, completely unnecessary. Look at people, look at that beautiful ass. Is it not a pleasure? I felt a hand glide over my butt and fiddle with my cunt. Slowly I was driven back and forth across the stage.

"Look at that pussy," cried the speaker and I felt my buttocks being pulled wide open. Two other hands joined in and also pulled my labia apart. The audience audibly enjoyed the spectacle. Then all hands released and I was driven a few meters further. There this game repeated itself and again, my ass and pussy were opened well for the crazy crowd. After the entire room was served like this, the speaker shouted: "Do you want to feel for yourself?" That last sentence barely dawned on me; I only felt that the goat I was stretched over was tilted slightly backwards so that my ass was lowered. Immediately I felt hands glide over my butt and feel my cat. I felt dozens of hands while driving back and forth. The audience almost fought to be in front. The fingers became more and more brutal and I regularly felt one trying to get inside. At one point, I felt a deep penetration almost immediately followed by a second one in my ass. This is going too far, I thought and feverishly, I tried to remember the code word. In the meantime, one finger after the other shot in at me. I just wanted to exclaim, or I was driven back to the middle under loud public shouts. My butt was glowing with the many chats and my pussy was a bit sore. Somewhere deep inside, I didn't even feel uncomfortable. My hands were released again. "Finished," I thought.

I was also allowed to use my legs to get up again and I was led back a bit unsteadily. The disappointment in the room was almost palpable and to my horror, I noticed that I actually thought it was a shame that it had ended. While I was still surprised by my own reaction, I heard a new, now familiar, sound: rolling wheels. It clearly wasn't over yet. A bit frightened and curious at the same time, I let myself be directed back to the center of the stage. The audience shouted again now that something else was going to happen.

Moreover, they could see what was coming. With a soft urge, I was forced to sit on a kind of plateau. Then I was pushed back so that I lay on my back with my lower legs dangling down. A sort of rod was placed over my stomach, against my hips and secured to the plateau. Now my legs were pushed up and folded around the bar until my feet tilted back and up. I lay now as if I was bent over with my knees bent, but then on my back. My ankles were again attached to something. Then I felt leather straps around my legs just above my knee. These were fixed and apparently, there were strings attached because now my knees were also pulled apart a little. My god, now I was very open — even worse than just on that goat. I still had some sense of protection there because I was standing with my back to the audience, now I lay wide-legged, knees raised in a kind of gynecologist's position. I felt like you could look into my womb. You could hear that from the audience.

The speaker again praised my wares, again completely

unnecessary. I had put my hands over my breasts, but that was not the intention. They were grabbed and pulled far apart to be detained there. Now imagine that you are crouching with your knees apart and with your arms outstretched as if you want to keep your balance. Then tilt your back on your back and you have a good idea of the position I was in now. But I am then fixed. This platform, of course, was able to turn, drive and even tilt and I soon noticed that I was being driven around and turned around again with loud cheers. Every spot was shown. To my own surprise, I started to like it. My mind, safe under the hood, began to feel like at a distance what the body was going through on the platform... and to like it...! A sudden swipe in volume from the audience pulled my attention back to the events. The speaker had done something that the audience apparently liked. I braced myself and felt something cold rolling over my breasts. The 'thing' was used by the speaker to mold my breasts. My feeling told me it was a smooth thing with a round point on it.

"Dildo, dildo," the audience chanted, confirming my suspicion. The speaker tilted the platform so that I was once again in a squat position. Then all parts of the room were allowed to see how my breasts were kneaded and massaged. After the round stage, I have tilted back again and you guessed it: the dildo found its way to my cat. Unconsciously I pushed my lower body forward towards the dildo. The speaker apparently saw it and immediately played it in "Oh oh gentlemen, what do we see here? Our main show is looking forward to it! Shall we help her?" "ERICA! ERICA!" was the room response. I immediately felt the dildo slip into my cunt. I could not help but have become so wet that the thing effortlessly popped in. The abundant oil made it even easier. For a moment, a thought shot through my mind: 'hello... you are lying here with your legs wide in front of an audience and a dildo publicly sews you! Wake up, that's not normal...! The thought ebbed away in horniness. I let myself be carried away by the audience and moved rhythmically with the dildo. I thought it was delicious. The speaker was absorbed in his activities; now, the audience excited him. After a while, I was about to cum. I didn't care more; I just thought about cummming. The presence of an audience only made me hornier. The idea that a room full of crazy guys watched me get peeled on stage with a dildo... The horny thing ran down my bottom. Through the horniness, I noticed at a certain moment that the dildo was no longer moving out of my cunt. He was pretty deep; if I wanted to, I couldn't express it. The roar from the room rose again. Something was about to happen again. I didn't even wonder anymore what; I just let it happen.

The code word occasionally floated by, but pure

horniness kept it at a distance. Then I felt something cold again. This time it pressed against my ass. I had hardly recovered from the shock or slowly, but surely I felt a second dildo penetrate my ass. Because of all the oil and horny juices from my cat, it was still very easy, but this was a novelty for me. However, I was so far gone that this could not scare me either. The dildo had a thickening halfway through and my ass had to stretch considerably to let it pass, but then it was stuck in it too. The room clapped and cheered. The speaker started to praise me again and I was again driven from left to right and back across the stage with those two dildos sticking out of my cunt and ass. The horny now just squeezed out past the dildos. I almost wanted to beg to get ready. The fat dildo in my cunt slowly slid outside, however hard I tried, I couldn't hold it. A loud disapproving cry came from the room. The speaker took the floor again. 'What is that now people? Can I just do that?' "No!" Do we have to do something about this?" "YES." "Forward lazy," the speaker called to the guards and I felt my cart almost pushed over the edge of the stage.

Moreover, I have tilted up again. If I could now take the hood off, I would oversee the entire room. Fortunately, I could not, because what I would have seen was the following: an outrageous crowd of roughly one hundred and one hundred and fifty men between the ages of twenty and thirty. There were also some women, at least in the first row.

Everyone forced themselves to stand at the front where I had driven. Behind me, the speaker had picked up the fallen dildo and given it to the nearest, outstretched hand. The lucky man fought further forward and screwed the dildo back into my cunt, not really gently. Immediately the waves hit horny again. Now the audience was allowed to sit one by one, the speaker announced. That was the signal for almost total chaos. As I was slowly being driven along the edge of the stage, I felt a cacophony of hands. The dildos were constantly pushed up and down, out and in, pussy and ass, my legs, belly and breasts were stroked, massaged and pinched.

My nipples turned and felt. Of course, the dildos were quickly compromised, but that was immediately resolved with fingers and hands. There were fingers in my cunt and ass, sometimes one but usually several and probably not even from the same hand. I wasn't even sure if they were fingers. I sunk into a drunken whirl of horniness and came on the assembly line. I had grown to sixty kilos of fuck meat, willing, horny — just a handle for my pussy and ass and ready for everything. When I reached the end of the stage and the last fingers were pulled out of my pussy and with a plop, the last object (?) Also left my ass, I wanted only one thing: more...! I heard a voice in my ear, "you are doing a fantastic job, baby. Do you want to go further?" I just nodded and wondered what the hell could mean 'even further.' "Ladies and gentlemen," the speaking master said, trying to regain control.

"Our main show has ended. Are you satisfied?" The answer was an enormous loud, consenting shout, peppered with dissatisfied 'more, more' callers. Probably the individual who had not managed to struggle forward in time. "Do you want another encore?!" "Yes," roared one hundred and fifty throats. "Do you really want an encore?" "Yes, we want more! We want more! We want more!"

"Ok then," the speaker cried, "Then I'm going to tell you that we will now park the main show in the MIDDLE OF THE STAGE and that from then on, sit will be FULLY at your disposal!" The roar rose to the pain threshold. In the meantime, I had been tipped completely back so that I was back on my back and apparently in the middle of the stage. The full implication didn't really dawn on me until I felt hands on my body again — multiple hands, dozens of hands, everywhere, everywhere, everywhere. My pussy, my ass, my breasts, my belly, thighs, mouth and face, even fingers and toes, everything was felt, pinched licked and penetrated. I sank even deeper into a blissful rush of indifferent horniness.

Somewhere far away, I noticed that the speaker and the guards were making sure everything went smoothly and that no one was hurting me. My pussy was empty for a moment but immediately and for the first time, filled with a penis and a solid one too. He pumped violently hard to and fro and my cart was almost pushed through his brakes. However, spraying soon and I felt how my cunt filled up. The cock had not been pulled out of me, or there was another one in it. In the meantime, my ass was constantly fingered. Another cock was pressed against my cheek and I opened my mouth to swallow it. These first dicks were apparently a kind of sign because apparently everyone now pulled out his cock. Everywhere I felt cocks rubbing past me and poking at me. They fought for a place in my pussy, ass, or mouth. I held my hands clasped like fists around, even more cocks that were getting ready. The hood over my head had already been soaked with sperm from the unlucky birds that couldn't get close enough and pulled away from me from a distance. My stomach and breasts and thighs were also full of sperm.

It ran in streams from my cunt and ass. I finished the assembly line. It seemed to last endlessly. A relentless parade of anonymous cocks pierced me and injected me. I just felt my buttocks and shoulders soaked in a puddle of cum. My mouth ran over. Sometimes I tried to swallow, but that didn't work out because the next dick penetrated my mouth again. My ass or pussy remained empty for a second. Big dicks, short dicks, long dicks, Lilliput dicks... the whole range came by and every hole that my body knew was penetrated. Sometimes I even had to catch my breath. I let it happen like unresisting fuck meat and enjoyed it. My mind was zero. Every dick that sprayed over me made me want more. I seemed insatiable. Suddenly my mouth was empty, but I felt something being pressed over it. Instinctively I felt with my tongue and discovered it was a cunt. So there were still women present!? I eagerly licked and pierced my seed-covered tongue as deeply as possible. I felt the cramp tighten and shockingly the woman came over me. Her juices ran down my chin and joined the sperm flasks under my head.

Immediately her place was taken again by a big dick. This went on and on. One cock after another occasionally interspersed with a pussy. After an infinite time in my experience, however, the latter had arrived. My pussy felt the last cock slip out of it and there was no more replacement, my ass felt no more rooting fingers and my mouth got stuck open... empty. What was left I was alone... completely fucked, still drunk with horniness. My brain registered how vaguely and from a distance I was. Lying on my back, knees pulled up and tied wide apart, my hands stretched out. My pussy soaked my ass too. Whole pee sperm in my navel, between my breasts, under my buttocks, shoulders and head. My face still covered with the sperm and pussy fluid hood. My arms, shoulders, thighs, feet and hands, breasts, everything was covered with a sticky layer of sperm. And I felt... wonderful.

My Lucky Day

Five more minutes, I thought to myself as I approached the door to my apartment. It had been a long day, and I was excited to finally get home and rest. With a certain pep in my step, I quickly withdrew my keys from my pocket and unlocked the door. As soon as my keys met the hole, a distinct and familiar barking met my ears. "Hush boy, I'm coming!" I called out to my companion, Anubis. Still, his barking continued to ring out as I finally pushed the door open. As I stepped over the threshold and into the apartment, I could hear him rounding the corner, running towards me. I couldn't help but smirk as I approached my favorite spot on the couch, eager to relax.

Right on cue, Anubis came barreling out of my bedroom, his nails clicking hurriedly against the hardwood floors. "Woah boy!" I called out, chuckling lightly as I looked at him. Before I could react, I felt the weight of his body against mine, pushing me back. I stumbled slightly, trying to regain my footing as I reached out for the couch to catch my fall, but it was no avail. With a gasp I fell to my knees, the wind knocked out of me from the push of his paws against my abdomen. I shook my head with a sigh, though my smile never leaving my face. I knew he wanted to play with me, and I couldn't fault him for that.

Anubis was quick to pounce on me, rearing up on his hind legs and bringing his upper body down on my back. It was clear that his intentions were to keep me on my knees, so I obliged. Leaning forward I positioned myself on my hands, waiting for Anubis to take note of my submission. It didn't take long before he rounded my body, bringing his groin near my face. I could already see his penis starting to extend from its sheath, pink, purple, and well sized. With a nod I lowered my head, letting him dominate me as he desired.

Without much hesitation Anubis adjusted his stance, pushing his pelvis forward, beckoning for my mouth. Without a moment's hesitation, I opened wide, letting the full length of him enter me. Right away he started to hump, thrusting forward and back in swift movements as I felt his well-sized member hitting the back of my throat. His paws pushed down firmly on my upper back and shoulders, keeping him well balanced as he pulsated inside my mouth. Reaching downwards with one hand I was able to swiftly undo the buttons and zipper adorning my pants. As I sucked gently atop of Anubis' erect member, I pushed my pants and undergarments downwards, well aware of what he would be wanting next.

In and out, in and out Anubis thrusted himself in my

mouth. His full length glided over my tongue and the roof of my mouth as he dominated me. I gasped trying to catch my breath as I felt my own cock hardening with anticipation. After several moments I pulled my head back, and closed my mouth, hoping to guide his interest elsewhere. Thankfully, as soon as my mouth was closed, Anubis took the hint. I could see his nose searching for my scent as he made his way behind me, and I lowered the upper part of my body towards the floor. With my ass lifted higher into the air, I inhaled deeply, waiting for Anubis to mount me.

Once again, I felt the weight of his paws on my lower back. His nails dug in lightly to my skin as he pushed forward, trying to find my hole. I took it upon myself to lick my hand and lubricate myself for him. He seemed grateful right away, letting out an audible yip as his member prodded against me. As I felt him find the right spot, I took a deep breath and closed my eyes. A few thrusts more and he was inside of me, his well-sized shaft pushing deep within me. I groaned with delight, feeling my cock throb with pleasure. With him inside of me, I could feel the fullness overtake my backside, urging me to enjoy myself.

Back and forth his pelvis started to move once more. With quick erratic thrusts he pulsated his hips back and forth, his paws held tight on either side of me. My heart was beating quickly in my chest, and my breath was heavy as I pushed back towards him, allowing him to penetrate me even deeper. My fingers curled into the hardwood, and my toes into the air as he dominated me, filling my entire hole with his throbbing erection. Mmm, I moaned quietly, feeling my cock pulse with pleasure. I knew that the harder and deeper he thrusted into me, the more I would milk upon the floor in front of me.

With great speed he continued thrusting, getting closer and closer to climax. His massive size held me down with ease as he bred me, his own erection throbbing with intense sensation inside of me. I could hear his breath getting heavy as he drew nearer to completion. I awaited feeling his knot swell inside me with great anticipation. All I could do was thrust back into him, hoping to bring him there faster as he pumped and pushed against me. My pre-cum dripped in droplets on the floor as my prostate was massaged by the full length and girth of his shaft.

Slowly but surely, I began to feel the sensation of him knotting up inside of me. He pumped with all his might, quickly swelling to the point that I knew he would not be able to pull out of me, even if he wanted to. With a few deep breaths, I thrusted back into him, urging him to continue. Within moments I felt his knot swell huge inside of me, filling me to the brim with his sheer girth. I groaned out loud as his wet, warm semen entered me, shooting deep inside of me. My body trembled with delight and my cock throbbed as he stayed beyond me, unable to pull away.

With him still firmly penetrating me, I reached downward, stroking my cock. I was able to shift my hips up and down, flexing my ass to continue massaging at my prostate, using his knot to aid me. The more I moved the more intense the pleasure became. I knew that if I just focused on the filling of his big, thick knot inside me, and the feeling of it pressing firmly against my prostate, that I would soon cum without having to jack myself off. A light sweat formed at my brow as I moaned and groaned, trying not to explode too quickly.

Still bent downwards in all fours I rocked myself from front to back and side to side. Anubis stayed on top of me, reminding me that I was submissive to him as his weight bared down upon my back. I groaned with pleasure as the head of my cock throbbed, warning me of what was coming. With a deep breath I pushed back against Anubis once more, and with that, I felt the semen explode from within me. It came forward swiftly and in great amounts, oozing down to the floor below me. Bit after bit it came, never seeming to stop as his knotted shaft milked me for every drop of semen I could muster.

The pleasure was so intense that I could feel the hairs

on my body standing on end. Just knowing that his wet, warm, semen was inside of me was enough to drive me wild. The more I moved on him, the more I came, and the more he filled me with his own juices. I knew that once we were finished, he would be stuck inside of me for some time, while his knot slowly started to go down. As tight as my ass was on top of him, If I continued to move, I could keep going for half an hour if not more. I had already come once, but the sensation of him milking the cum from my cock without it even being touched was one I reveled in.

Only after there was nothing left to give, and his knot had finally dissipated did he slowly pull out of me. I rolled my eyes back with a final groan as I felt shaft slide out of me, leaving my ass dripping with his cum. As I stood slowly, I could see our semen mixing together, glossy and wet against the hardwood floor. I couldn't help but grin as I looked down upon it, still trying to catch my breath, and come down from the height of sensation and pleasure. "Good boy Anubis," I said, reaching out to lightly stroke his head. With a smile and a deep breath, I pointed towards my bedroom, my tone soft as I continued to speak to him. "Go get in the bed, I'll clean up this mess."

The Substitute Teacher

It was the last class of the week, and so far my time had passed quite well. As a young and quite pretty substitute teacher I was used to badly disciplined school children with constant barbs about my shapely stupid blonde appearance. Dealing with the hooligan dynasty of alpha males and spiteful females trying to maintain their dominance was also a further prerequisite for survival. If nothing, then it considered me mean and harsh on the outside, even if I flinched on the inside. The jealous looks of the girls I taught, knowing that their friends wanted me more than they did, were also a constant in every class that I tried to control as much as I could. I was quite small and slightly overweight compared to the more marriageable cheerleaders in the class. Since I was only twenty-three years old, it seemed more like curvature than anything else. Unfortunately, despite my rather large bottom, I was quite flat-chested, and on those days when I was only filling in for other teachers, I didn't see any downside in filling out my bra to make me look stronger and more intimidating. I could handle teasing about my bottom, but since I was a teenager, I was very sensitive about my lack of cleavage. I must say that I cut an impressive figure with an accentuated bust, my light cream power suit and my red 4-inch heels. Even though I didn't always like some of the ruder comments that were often put in my way, if I'm honest, I knew I could have discouraged them with more.

Anyway, that Friday I found myself in a fairly upper middle-class high school in a mid-sized town in my home state of California. I had gone to high school there and was only a twenty-minute drive from my new apartment. It was my dream to find a permanent job here, and with my college debts growing exponentially, it was almost a necessity. Some of the staff remembered me from my time here as a rather uncouth favorite student, and certainly Principal Harding appreciated me very much, although he might have preferred to remember me in my cheerleading outfit rather than my more elegant business suit. During the lunch break, I caught one of the older girls in my current class shitting the pants of a classmate and informed the principal. As a former victim of such pranks, I had no mercy for the perpetrator. I hoped that she would get into trouble and assumed that she would be given an immediate suspension so that I would not have to deal with her again as she had a rather scary appearance. So I was quite surprised to see her strolling into my last class and approaching me calmly, almost reluctantly.

"I am so sorry for the former Miss Gatting. It will never happen again. Please take this cup of coffee as a token of truce and no hard feelings. I know what I did was wrong and I hope that you can forgive me. Papa called me a terrible name..."

Papa? What did she mean by that? I was looking at my class list of names. I looked at my class list. The girl's name was Sylvia, Sylvia Harding, and she must be Principal Harding's daughter. Oh, God, how could I be so stupid as to think that that wouldn't have improved my chances of getting a permanent job or even a reference. So, in an effort to reconcile, I graciously accepted the cup of coffee, even though I neither drank coffee nor even liked it.

"Well, that's really a lovely gesture, Sylvia. I must say I was a little tired, so a cup of coffee should really cheer me up. Thank you, my dear, I hope you didn't go to too much trouble," I replied and tried to ingratiate myself with her.

When I took a sip of the coffee, I thought it tasted strange, but when she looked up at me excitedly, I looked down at her and nodded my appreciation. Within five minutes, thank God, I had drunk the whole cup and was able to get through my last lesson of the day comfortably. Everyone seemed to have behaved remarkably well so far, and I even began to relax a little and enjoy the lesson.

Then, about ten minutes after the class started, I felt a strange fullness in my stomach. As I stood at the blackboard trying to explain the relevance of the Canterbury tales to a disinterested bunch of teenagers, I suddenly felt a big pile up in my stomach. I stumbled briefly and could feel that the class noticed my discomfort. I tried to ignore it, but thirty seconds later the fullness gave way to a stronger cramping pain in my stomach. I felt the increase in pressure in my stomach and struggled to my stool to get a temporary respite. But it was no use. The pressure pushed down through my intestine and the cramps became almost unbearable. The urge to empty my bowels was insatiable. I knew immediately that something terrible would happen if I didn't get out of this classroom soon. I tried to stay as calm as possible, turned to the door and told the class that I would be back in a minute. I could feel their giggle and reuse as I stumbled, sweat building up on my forehead towards the door. I knew I didn't have much time as I turned the door handle before I was planning to flee madly down the hallway to the bathroom.

It no longer bothered me that over twenty-five pairs of eyes from eighteen-year-old students, all senior high school students, witnessed my embarrassing escape. But when I let the door come back towards me to open it, I realized that it would not move. For five desperate seconds I pushed and pulled desperately and without success, while the class became more and more lively as they watched my curious escapades. My need to defecate was overwhelming and as I looked back at the class, I could see that Sylvia was almost unimpressed by the madness of her classmates and the panic that emanated from me unabatedly. She was the only one who didn't seem surprised by my irrational behavior. Another convulsive tremor flowed through my body, and only with intense physical will could I prevent the fatal faucal accident from happening. Finally, and with a devastating feeling of fear, I knew that I could not hold out much longer. I realized that someone had locked the door and asked for a key, but while the words were still leaving my mouth, another wave was seeping through my system.

"PLEASE, SOME HELP..." I cried out in horror as the reality of what was happening quickly dawned on me in class, when a horrible, elongated, flatulent event echoed from my rear end, drowning out even the loudest laughter in the class.

A vibrating fart bursting into decibels echoed wildly from my big ass. Only with my greatest willpower could I stop the fart before it changed from gaseous to semi-solid form. Nonetheless, this anal eruption made the class laugh, and it was clear that I would not get any sympathy from these teenage hyenas. Although it was only a fart, I knew I could not hold back the insidious forces that were holding my body hostage for much longer. Whatever was inside me was determined to leave, and with great reluctance I knew that the class would probably get a show they would never forget. Bizarrely, in the half seconds before the ultimate anal explosion, I resignedly debated in immense existential despair whether or not I would perform the nasty deed in my pants and make a massive mess of my clothes, or squat on the floor and empty myself on the floor. Neither, of course, was appealing. When I realized that I would have to leave the building later in some kind of clothes, I made the humiliating decision to quickly slip my suit trousers and panties over my ankles and squat in an inelegant manner in front of the class. This humiliating act brought the boys a primal spasm and the girls a hideous grin. Unfortunately, I didn't really hold my own down there. My blond bush was quite wild, and even in spite of the enormous situation I found myself in, there was still a clever Alec boy commenting on something ridiculous, which caused even more derisive laughter. So I squatted in my 4-inch heels, naked pussy and ass, which were displayed to over twenty children, and waited in disgust while a last, all-encompassing, throbbing and viscous wave of pain went through me until finally I could not stand it any longer. When I looked up, I noticed that by now all the kids had left their seats, and they followed my dirty demonstration in deepest excitement from all imaginable angles. They knew that they were witnessing something truly monumental.

When the resistance of my sphincter finally eased, I could feel an almost volcanic eruption shooting out of me. Some children from behind could actually see the poop lifting off my butt and starting its long fall to the floor, while others in front watched my trembling, sweaty face with tears falling down as I contorted mercilessly while aware of the exhibition I was offering. Only then did I see the multitude of telephone cameras, even a video camera, all of which caught me at an unflattering angle, and although I knew it was a terrible view, I did not want my naked image to be broadcast while I was performing this most evil of acts. So in a moment of madness I reached for my panties, and when the first elongated turd fell off my butt without further ado, I tore up my white cotton panties, caught the excrement in mid-flight and pulled them back up towards my still gushing butt. When it came in contact with my butt, it rubbed and squeezed itself around my now freshly covered butt. The smell was foul and the scene was relentless.

Unfortunately for me, the shit just kept coming back. Within seconds the panties filled up and almost unnaturally I felt that my now destroyed panties were full to the brim and the feces like riverbanks at high water flooded my panties in all directions. I was amazed at the sheer volume and speed of the action, for I am sure it was the bound schoolchildren.

The sinister look of disgust and ridicule continued when, after a short pause for breath, another massive surge of electricity came out of my anus. This time the discharge of excrement was so violent and explosive that even as I squatted there in my four-inch high heels, with my hands on either side of my cramped stomach, the sheer volume of faeces made my panties slide down my legs, leaving a brown, dirty trail. When they landed on my ankles, I knew immediately that they had destroyed my cream-colored pants, but that was the least of my worries at the moment.

The scene was unbearable. All these people stared in macabre fascination at their teacher, who humiliated herself in such a horrible way. Again, I saw the cameras pointed at my crotch and my bottom, which was now, of course, covered with an unbearable chocolate mess. The sheer volume was staggering, and finally it seemed as if the river, which had long been beyond my control, had come to a halt. My face begged for mercy, my mouth was incapable of speaking, while the bodies and cameras of my students around me pressed around their positions. The sound of flashes and giggles from the class continued until one boy held his camera almost directly under my crotch. I immediately clasped my hands to my stained pussy, hoping to fruitlessly fend off these photographic intruders. No sooner had I done that than I realized my mistake. The poop was frozen to my once blonde pubic hair, and when I touched it with my hands now, a big sticky mass ran onto my fingers. I looked down in horror, as if the events that were taking place were a nightmare, but as this was accompanied by further shockulence, I saw a camera in my face capturing my broken emotional state. Again, almost unconsciously I tried to shield my face as if the images had not already said a thousand words of humiliation. I put my hands in front of my face and as soon as I did so, my grave mistake became clear to me. The smell was obscene, but when I blocked my face with my hands, a volume of poop splashed over my once beautiful complexion. The make-up I had been wearing, already discolored by tears, was now drowning in the soft, sticky excrement from my intestines. Instead of protecting my face, I smothered it in my foul-smelling brew. More photos were taken and even more atavistic laughter was captured from the audience who, if they had once felt pity, were now completely immersed in my horrible ordeal. Still squatting, I tried to stand up, thinking my bowels could certainly not produce more, but when I bent my stomach to hear another original rumble from behind, it squeaked out. This time the contents were looser and gushed out painfully in one quick burst that lasted no longer than three seconds. But the effect was undeniable. A scatological spray formed like a puddle under my writhing body.

From the crowd of teenagers further collective cries of disgust were heard. The pain in my stomach began to subside and I looked down at my dirty panties, my legs and ankles, and the feelings of humiliation were overwhelming. I wanted to be somehow clean so that I could hide from the relentless looks. I rubbed my dirty hands off my sky-blue blouse to somehow free them from their impotence. Unfortunately, all I did was unknowingly leave another brown trace on my blouse. Everything I did was recorded, and every move I made was accompanied by the sound of "UGH!" and "GROSS!" or a variation of them.

In the midst of all this chaos, I once again encountered the bright light of Sylvia Harding, who seemed calmer than all the others, much like a peaceful lioness watching other lions tearing up scraps of meat. But in her eyes, I saw a serenity that I needed, and in my humiliating paralysis I felt that maybe she could offer me a break from this situation.

Almost instantly she jumped out of her chair and in an instant, she divided the crowd in front of me and looked down on me with something I felt was between pity and disgust.

"My goodness, what a mess you've made. Don't just stand there and admire your dirty work, why don't you at least try to cover your dirty vagina with the suit jacket?

I still felt paralyzed, but amazingly the girl stepped behind me and almost involuntarily she slid the shoulders of my suit jacket over my flaccid arms and back. In one quick movement she wrapped the suit jacket around the front of my upper body. She was right; at least my front was covered, even though my bottom was still completely exposed. Maybe she was trying to help.

"Now do exactly as I say and this nightmare will soon be over," she whispered to me.

I obeyed as in hypnosis. Suddenly the laughter of the crowd in my head stopped and for a while I only heard the voice of Sylvia who helped me out of my crisis. I nodded submissively and when she ordered me to take off my blouse, since I had destroyed it with my dirty hands, I couldn't help but obey her. Slowly I opened the blouse and wiped even more shit from my hands while pressing the buttons. Finally I had taken off the blouse and looked at Sylvia for further instructions. She told me to throw it in the corner of the room and as I did so

I heard another collective "OOH!

Now only dressed in a bra and with a jacket wrapped around her crotch, I looked at Sylvia for further instructions.

"Oh my God! Is your bra padded or what? I'm sure I can see that there's paper hidden in your bra," she asked almost rhetorically.

I was too stunned to answer, I just looked down and could only slightly see the paper loop hanging loosely from my ruffled oversized bra, but I couldn't believe that in the midst of all the other hustle and bustle she would have noticed it so quickly. My stunned expression and my guilty behavior were answer enough for Sylvia.

"You're lucky you have something to wipe your dirty ass with MsSCATing," Sylvia announced as she dug her hands into my bra and like a magician pulled paper out of one sleeve and unfolded the huge rolls of paper until my bra hung listlessly and loosely from my body.

I wondered if she was calling me Miss Scating for a moment as I complied with her request.

When she handed me the bundled toilet paper that gave me confidence, she ordered me to clean myself.

I knew that what I was doing was ridiculous, but I was still trapped in the room, and since I had no other options, I just stuck to the one person who seemed to have authority. Still on my heels, the lower half of my body covered with poop, my face grazed too much, as if I had just had a poop facial, but my upper body only with traces. My white bra and my white body offered a strong contrast to all this. I crouched down to wipe my bottom and as I did so, the suit jacket slipped off and revealed my smudged front again. Once again exposed I tried to follow Sylvia's orders when she told me to ignore my nakedness. Unfortunately, despite the toilet paper I didn't make much progress in the mess I had made. I tipped the dirty cloth on the floor in the stinking puddle of excrement where I was standing.

As a variety of thoughts flashed through my mind, including how I might ever get home or even get clean or get over this incident, I felt Sylvia unhook my bra in the back... "You're still dirty...need something else to clean yourself...hmmm, how about this thing, it doesn't seem to work anymore.

Crazy, despite all I had been through, I still felt humiliated because of my not very luscious breasts. On another day it would have been a shattering experience if I had been discovered that I had falsified my appearance as I had been. It shouldn't have mattered in connection with the last fifteen minutes, but when I submissively started to remove my bra from my body, I wished the bottom could have opened up and swallowed me right there. Instead, more people than ever before got an unencumbered view of my naked breasts as in the midst of a fresh round of quick-tempered and angry laughter and the dots, glances and flashing cameras I tried to use my bra to wipe my dirty bare bottom clean.

In each cup I scooped a large amount of the sticky, smelly substance. My hands were now completely brown, as the excess was matting on my skin. I couldn't believe that I had wiped my butt completely naked in a classroom full of students after I had performed the most private of all actions right in front of their eyes.

"OH MY GOD, THIS IS THE MOST REVOLVING THING I EVER SEE", exclaimed just one of the many voices that penetrated the crowd.

"AND OH MY GOD, LOOK AT HER TINY TITS. I CAN'T BELIEVE I THOUGHT I THAT THAT BITCH WHAT HOT!', cried another voice.

How humiliating and for some reason the barbs on my tiny breasts still hurt deeply. Maybe I should cover them, I thought to myself, and almost in post-traumatic shock I tried to adapt the dirty bra back to my body. Immediately I felt the poop being squeezed against my breasts and dripping into my stomach. Sylvia looked at me with dismay.

"This is just disgusting, if you want to leave this classroom, I suggest you take this oversized bra made of poop off your body. I mean really, just look at the mess you've made of your clean and perverted little bosom. It seems to me that you must have a scat fetish or something," said Sylvia, leaving me little choice but to take the bra off again and let it fall to the floor so that now a boob covered with steaming poop appears.

"Luckily, my dad gave me the key to school, so why don't I escort you to the locker room and you can borrow this... "and you can wash that dirt off the body. I mean, oh my God, look at you, you're fucking disgusting now, right? Now take off your dirty panties and pants and we can take care of it!"

I couldn't help feeling the disgusting taste when I wiped them with my hands so dirty. She was right, I was disgusting, but when my mind gained temporary clarity, I thought why the door was locked, why, if she had a key, she didn't try to open the door earlier.

"Stop hesitating and take it off at once," she moved again and threw those thoughts out of her head again.

Anyway, the task wasn't so easy in four-inch heels and standing in a puddle of excrement. I knew I had to take off my heels to get the job done, but I didn't want to stand barefoot in my own mess, so I was hoping briefly to be able to take the dirty clothes off my feet while I was still wearing my heels. So I stood my left foot on half the clothes and quickly raised my right foot to do the job. This turned out to be even harder than I imagined, and as I jumped from foot to foot trying to take off the dirty clothes, I saw my whole body vibrate wildly. If I had big breasts, I would know they would be swaying madly now, but when I suddenly released the left side of my panties and pants from my left heel, a new swing made me lose balance with my right and slipped, as if on ice, first face the pelvis below. The consistency of this looser, more liquid pile was quickly washed all over my body when I hit the ground, practically swimming. The front of my body was now completely covered with various shades of brown, including the face, and while I was soaking in the search for air, I tossed my body on my back to open my mouth to the air. Lying there in what was now a complete humiliation, I looked up at Sylvia, who was rising above me. She was now laughing mercilessly at me and I saw evil in her eyes. And then he hit me almost like a stone between my eyes, as bright as day. Coffee, keys...